Kelly lifted her chin. "I'm going to tell you something, Todd Richardson. Someday you and Robbie are going to be friends."

I stared at her as if she were crazy. Robbie had everyone wrapped around his little finger. Was I missing something somewhere?

"Very good friends," she said, pulling on her coat. "You wait. It's going to happen."

"Never," I said after she left. I chomped down on another cookie. "I'll never forgive him for taking you away from me."

MARGOT B. McDONNELL lives in Scottsdale, Arizona, with her husband and their four children. *My Own Worst Enemy* is her first novel.

OTHER PACER BOOKS YOU WILL ENJOY:

My Own Worst Enemy

MARGOT B. McDONNELL

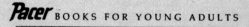

Pacer BOOKS FOR YOUNG ADULTS

B®

BERKLEY BOOKS, NEW YORK

This Berkley/Pacer book contains the complete
text of the original hardcover edition.

MY OWN WORST ENEMY

A Berkley/Pacer Book, published by arrangement with
the author

PRINTING HISTORY
Pacer/Putnam edition / October 1984
Berkley/Pacer edition / November 1985

ISBN: 0-425-08425-6
RL: 4.9

Pacer is a trademark belonging to
The Putnam Publishing Group.

For Ian

He who has a thousand friends has not a friend to spare,
And he who has one enemy shall meet him everywhere.
                    —Emerson

Chapter

1

I was looking through my high school yearbook a few days ago, and I started remembering when I was sixteen, in love, in hate and in trouble. I can't believe that in two weeks I, Todd Richardson, will be a freshman at Stanford University and the gang from East Powell High will be splitting up.

Rick's off to Arizona State and Walt's driving semis cross-country. Who knows if I'll ever see Diane again? With beautiful Kelly Small, the love of my life, headed for New York, I can't help but wonder what's in store for us.

And then there's Robbie Samson, the best friend I ever had—and the most mysterious. When I think of Robbie now, I get that incredible feeling of wanting something so badly but at the same time knowing it won't work out. It's like never being able to forget the easy grounder you flubbed in the biggest game of the year. Or the brilliant remark for the best-looking girl in school that came into your head five minutes after she left. You know—everybody goes through it.

If I had proved myself to Robbie as a friend, what I'm about to write might have had a different ending. Once in a while when I think of him, which is still often, considering it's been more than a year and a half since I've seen him, I can't remember what he looks like unless I get out the picture Mom took of him and me. I'll never forget his eyes, though. He guarded those eyes with everything he had until the day he decided to trust me. Then he really confided in me. And I understood.

The irony of all of this is that before Robbie became the best friend I ever had, he was my worst enemy.

The first time I saw Robbie a lot of guys were standing around in the gym waiting to get their sports fitness checkups. I knew most of the boys from over the years, even though East Powell High had 1800 students, but a few had changed during the summer.

One kid had grown at least five inches and croaked every time he opened his mouth. Rick, my closest friend, had developed a severe case of acne and complained when he had to take off his T-shirt in front of everybody. I thought about myself. Why wasn't I growing? My voice had changed, but I was still 5' 6", while the girl of my dreams had already hit 5' 7". Also, my dad had been bald for a long time. I could see myself at thirty—short, fat and hairless, like Dad.

After the doctor had weighed and measured me, I

went across the gym to put on my jeans and shirt. On the way I saw Robbie standing apart from the others. He had all his clothes on and held a bottle out in front of him as if he didn't know what to do with it.

What a jerk, I thought, and called to Rick, who was lacing up his sneakers. At the time, Robbie's looks didn't make the slightest impression on me. After we knew each other I asked him once, "Was that you in the gym that day holding the bottle of pee?" He grinned. "And were you that runty blond doing all those dumb handstands?"

Robbie stood at least four inches taller than I. We were opposites to the extreme. His hair was almost black and mine was the color of grapefruit juice. He had the kind of skin that tanned in a day, while my face held contests with my arms to see which could sprout the most freckles. My eyes were such a pale blue that they looked gray sometimes, and Robbie's were so dark you couldn't see the pupils. I had duck feet. His knees and toes met each other politely when he walked, his legs long and underdeveloped, except for his front thighs. He had a thin body, too bony for wrestling and football. His feet and hands were enormous, like a half-grown animal's.

Nearly three months later I met him. On the days Rick and I didn't have basketball practice he and I went to the DQ or hung around Wally's and read the *Playboys* and sports magazines. One December afternoon we crunched through the snow, our spirits cold and dreary as the weather, moaning about life's injustices. Rick's skin condition was making him paranoid and I had barely survived the worse trauma of my life—losing Kelly.

No one can tell you unrequited love is easier on guys. It's disaster. We try to stay cool while our insides are disintegrating.

"I must have screwed up somewhere," I muttered. "I don't understand it."

"At least you had a girlfriend," Rick said. "Look at me. Who'd want someone with a face like mine?"

"You're better off," I said. "Your face will clear up. My love life won't."

"Come on, Todd!"

"Hey, I'm sorry." Rick did look terrible—his face, I mean. The rest of him was perfect, the muscles, height. He was the only guy our age I knew who already had hair on his chest. He played every sport well. I wouldn't have minded a few of his better qualities.

I heard a noise behind us. Rick glanced back. "It's Kelly," he said under his breath, "with *him*."

I looked at Rick. "Who is he?"

"His name is Robbie Samson. He's new. From Chicago, I think."

A snowball hit me in the back of my head. Whirling around, I saw him then, a skinny, black-haired kid wearing a ridiculous knitted cap and a wide crooked grin that took up most of his face.

"What do you think you're doing?" I yelled. Wiping wet snow from my hair, I glared at Robbie. He held Kelly's hand. I felt like breaking all his fingers.

"How're you doing, Kelly?" Rick said, a few steps behind me.

Kelly's mouth turned up in a mischievous smile. "Todd," she said, "I'm the one who threw it."

I couldn't think of a thing to say. He had to be at least 5′ 10″. Why did he have to hold her hand? She stood next to him in her fur-topped boots and ski jacket, her cheeks dimpled and pink in the chilly afternoon.

I turned to Rick. "I'm going home," I said, shoving my hands into my pants pockets and leaving the three of them. I didn't want to look back at that disgusting smirk.

"Wait a minute," Kelly said. "I want you to meet Robbie."

I walked back. "Hi," he said, sticking out his hand. I kept mine planted. "We're in the same algebra class, I think. Don't you sit up front?" I nodded. "I'm way in back."

Where you should be. I'd never noticed him in there, but it was a big class.

"Todd's a brain," Kelly said, patting my arm.

Long on brains, short in stature. Miserably, I noticed how well Kelly's height suited Robbie's. She could have picked someone better-looking, though.

"He'll win a scholarship for sure," she added.

"And you'll cinch the Miss Universe contest," Robbie said.

"Ha!" Kelly said, laughing. "I plan to do something meaningful with my life."

I thought of all the "meaningful" things I had fantasized doing with her. She would have been angry if she knew what they were.

I've seen tender looks before, but the mush that passed between Kelly and Robbie made me want to puke. I couldn't force one word out of my mouth. Why hadn't Kelly told me about all of this?

"I have to go," I finally got out.

"See you 'round," Robbie said, half smiling.

I hope not. "Yeah," I said. "Bye, Kelly."

Rick and I started down the road. "They were holding hands," he said when we were a block away.

"No," I said. "For crying out loud, do you think I'm blind?"

"Think they're going together?"

"How would I know? I don't care. Let them. And shut up, will you? Anyone can hold hands."

"Sure, but don't try to hold mine, okay?"

Chapter
2

We walked the rest of the way to my house in silence, and I thought of how long I'd known Kelly—practically my whole life, though the first time I talked to her wasn't until the day I wet my pants in the fourth grade and cried halfway through recess. I always knew who she was, but at that age girls just weren't important.

That day so long ago I was sitting behind a hedge, hoping for dried pants before the bell rang, when Kelly peeked around the bush at me. She had a chubby body, fat blond braids and teeth that made her face look like a beaver's.

"Get out of here," I cried, rubbing my runny nose.

"My brother has clothes," she said. "He won't care if you borrow some."

"No," I said, placing my hands over the evidence, "we're not supposed to leave the school grounds."

"I live across the street. We'll come right back."

After she found me an old pair of shorts, I went back to school. Even then she knew how to make everything right.

We hardly talked again until junior high, because the next year Kelly moved across town. I didn't recognize her when she skipped up to me the first day, a tall slender girl whose teeth now fit her mouth. Her hair was streaky blond, and something engrossing had happened to her chest.

My life took both a wonderful and a terrible turn that day. Wonderful: I fell in love. Terrible: I didn't know what to do about it. Pretty soon I had joined every club she belonged to except Tri-Y, which is for girls only, and I usually managed to show up where she hung out without being too obvious.

Nothing happened.

My big break came the summer after eighth grade, when baseball season was over and Rick and I were rattling around trying to find something to do. A friend of my mother, who was the director of Camp Cherokee in River Falls, asked me to be game leader for two months, to replace a guy who had had an emergency appendectomy.

A few days later, after a tetanus shot and a crash course in first aid, I boarded the bus and surveyed thirty-five hyper ten-year-olds trying to bounce the stuffing out of their seats.

"I must have been crazy to say yes," I said, ducking a pair of swim fins sailing through the air.

Then I spotted Kelly.

"What are you doing here?" I said, rushing to the back of the bus.

She laughed. "What are *you* doing here? I'm a counselor. You too?"

I nodded and sat down beside her. Two months with Kelly Small. I settled back in the seat, oblivious to the noise, wondering how I got so lucky.

After one day at camp, I understood why I loved her. Everyone else did, too. She got the kids to sing at the top of their lungs while she pranced among them. Since she'd been at Camp Cherokee before, she knew the crafts and taught us how to make those woven plastic key rings, macrame plant hangers and pot holders.

By the end of the first week she had a deep tan that made her green eyes shine as we sat and sang around the campfire. I never liked marshmallows until Kelly cooked me a burnt one. "Open up," she said, and it tasted great because she fed it to me.

She and I spent a lot of time together that summer, I guess since we were friends to begin with. Other guys took her sailing, but she liked to walk and swim with me. Sometimes after the kids went to sleep we crept out of our cabins and went down to the lake. We did that the last night, and I had this welled-up, half-excited, half-panicked feeling that I didn't want to go back to East Powell at all.

"In two weeks we'll be high school freshmen. Can you believe it?" she asked, taking my hand. "Are you nervous?"

Yeah, I thought, but not about that. I wanted to kiss

her so much that I was getting dizzy thinking about it. After all, we were alone. The moonlight shimmered on the lake water and made her hair gold. The setting was perfect.

Then she turned to me and smiled. "Let's always be friends," she whispered. "I've had such a good time up here with you."

She was close to me, and I smelled her hair—soap and campfire. I wanted to tell her how I felt at that moment, but I couldn't even get started. Before I knew it, she had grabbed my arm and pulled me into the water, where we laughed and splashed each other until the director came down and told us to go back to our cabins.

The next year floated by. Kelly and I saw each other, but it wasn't the same. She was everyone's friend and I couldn't get up the nerve to call her for a real date, even though we talked and joked around a lot. At the end of the year she gave me her school picture. I kept it by my bed. When summer came she went back to Camp Cherokee all three months, while I helped my grandpa on his farm. I wrote her four or five times, but either my letters didn't get there or she didn't have time to write me. Anyway, she didn't mention them when we got back to school.

Three weeks before the snowball incident a miracle happened. Kelly invited me home for dinner. "You mean me?" I asked like a dying patient who's just been told he's going to live after all.

The evening was uncomfortable. My tie went into the orange sauce and I blew it trying to talk intelligently to

Kelly's father. But later, when Kelly and I took a walk in the snow, I somehow found the courage to put my arm around her, and she let me. It was perfect.

Like a salmon swimming upstream, I braved blizzards to see her every day. I walked her to class and called her every night. At the end of the week I asked her to go to a dance at East with me.

"Why not?" she said, squeezing my hand.

I was in heaven for seven whole days.

Saturday she called me. "A boy asked me out," she said. "I don't think you know him. He's new. Anyway, he won't let me say no."

"Just say no."

"You and I are still friends. After all, he and I are only going ice skating."

My throat stuck to itself. "Have him find a date. We'll double."

"He wants to go with me. It'll be all right." Kelly's voice got quiet. "Todd, we both have a right to be with others, you know."

"You can if you want."

I worried about it all weekend. Monday she told me this person needed help with some class. Tuesday he asked her skating again and I began to face my suspicions. This Lone Ranger from Chicago had moved in and taken her away from me, just when I was beginning to make real progress.

When Rick and I reached my house, I saw Pete Kawolczyk pulling up in his truck from A & L Body Parts, which looked like it was ready for the junk heap.

"Had an hour to kill," he called, getting out. "How are you two doing?"

"Hi, Pete," Rick said, glancing at me.

Pete was almost a part of our family. My dad has zero mechanical ability, and one winter while he was driving home from Madison on a back road, something dropped off the engine. If Pete hadn't come along, my dad might have frozen to death. Dad insisted that Pete come over for dinner the next week, and he ended up staying late, talking sports with Dad and telling jokes. Before he left, the two had set a date to go hunting together.

That happened when I was nine and Pete was nineteen. After that, Pete kept our cars running. My mother invited him over for dinner now and then, and as I got older I got to go hunting with him and Dad. In the last few years my dad had become too busy at his insurance agency to take any time off, and now Pete was more or less my friend alone.

"Todd boy, you look like you got run over," Pete said. "What's up?"

"He's pissed," Rick said as we went into the house.

"Shut up, Rick." I walked to the kitchen counter. "My mom made some cake," I said. "Help yourselves, if you want."

"I was thinking maybe I could fix you up this weekend," Pete said. "There's this new band playing over in Galesburg. Interested?"

"Pete, you don't have any sixteen-year-old girlfriends," I said.

"No, but one of them is bound to like sixteen-year-old boys."

"No thanks."

Rick laughed, spewing crumbs all over the place. "You're always talking about Galesburg."

"Someday you're going to one of those dances," Pete assured us. "It's time you guys learned what's what."

"Maybe when I'm older," I told Pete. "Right now I'm not sure I'm—"

"Haven't I known you since you were a mere peanut? Haven't I?"

"Yes, but—"

"Believe me, it's time."

"I don't think Todd's ready for adventure just now. There's this girl—"

I glared at Rick.

"Uh, sorry, old buddy. Okay if I pour myself some milk?"

"Is that all that's bothering you?" Pete asked me. "*One* girl? Does a bachelor stick to one girl?"

"She and I were going together, Pete, and all of a sudden—"

Pete raised his hand. "You don't have to say a thing. I've heard it before. I've lived it. Women sometimes like to keep guys dangling. It's part of their nature. Don't worry about it."

"That may be true," Rick said, sticking his head into the refrigerator, "but in this case, Todd's got to face that she has another boyfriend on the horizon."

"Drop it," I said.

"Who is it?"

I left the kitchen before I had to hear that name again.

Chapter

3

I saw him the next day in the cafeteria, where I worked during lunch as a food server. Most of the time I dished up mashed potatoes or vegetables. Today it was corn. I despised standing in back of the counter every day wearing an apron, but my dad thought it was good experience, so I went along with it.

Halfway through the lunch period I saw him come in alone and get in line. He had on a pair of brown cords and a skintight navy sweater without a shirt under it. No one at East wore sweaters without shirts.

When he reached me, he gave me a lopsided grin. "Oh hi," he said. "What a cute apron."

"Thanks. I made it in home ec," I said.

"Put a lot of corn on there, will you? It's my favorite." I shoveled some extra in the empty space. "Come on," he said, holding up the line, "can't you do any better than that? I'm *starved*."

I don't know what made me do it, but I scooped up two giant spoonfuls and dumped them right on top of his Salisbury steak and peaches. "How's that?" I asked.

"Much better," he said, walking off to the milk station.

I could have grabbed his tray and hit him over the head with it. Where did he get off demanding special service? Diane, who was dishing out meat, poked me into action again.

After school I went to see Mom at Best's department store, where she worked. She used the money she made to finance classes she took while Dad worked late almost every night.

"Is she in?" I asked the woman who ran the register.

"She's with a customer," she said. "How's school, Todd?"

"Okay." Why did everyone always ask about school? I shifted around, wondering what I was doing standing in a sea of ladies' underwear.

My mother came out with a big smile on her face and a tape measure around her neck. "Todd, what a treat," she said. I could tell she wanted to hug me, but I played dumb and looked at a rack of robes. For some reason Mom had gotten clingy lately. Dad pushed me away and Mom tried to pull me back. "I just pinned up five hems and let out two seams," she said. "Fascinating work. How much money do you need?"

"I didn't come for money." I had had to admit to that motive several times in the past, but not today.

"Okay, what's up?" She didn't push me to talk unless I started to. My dad was all right most of the time, too, as long as he didn't go on about his insurance business. I overheard my parents talking one night, saying that our family doctor had told my father he would need a bypass operation soon. I wasn't about to worry him with anything I had on my mind. I wasn't even sure why I had come to see my mother. I mean, how do you tell your own mother you'd like to kill someone because he smiled at you? My mom was into that golden rule stuff. At the moment, my interpretation of "do unto others" was to cram crap down the throat of whoever issued the same unto you.

"I just came by," I mumbled. "Guess I'll go." I had nothing to say but a lot I wanted to say. You can tell a person that he shouldn't judge, but no one can ever know another's insides, and I couldn't change my growing anger toward Robbie Samson if God Himself told me to.

I walked along in the dim light of late afternoon. About two blocks from my house I began to think about how things were in junior high when all of us were around the same height. I picked up some snow and started pitching snowballs—baseballs and footballs really—at a telephone pole, remembering how I had played every sport and how my friends used to say I was the best shooter on the basketball team.

Girls liked me, too, and Rick and I took football honors. I even received the all-athlete award over Rick, and that summer he and I went to State with the Senior League All-Stars baseball team.

I guess it was stupid of me to believe I'd stay on top of

the pile. When I entered East, nothing happened. Boys who had been clumsy got coordinated and passed me in ability. My friends inched up. Mom told me nothing stays the same, but I didn't believe her since I sure was staying the same size. Dad said the same thing had happened to him. So I began to study. What else was there? I had to be superior in something. Now, instead of being known as Joe Jock, I became a brain.

Mom was happy but told me I didn't have to be perfect. Dad tried to convince me I was scholarship material. My friend Pete made one comment: "Get your butt out on the baseball field."

Being short didn't hurt my ball playing. As they say, when you're close to the ground, it's easier to catch the ball. I could run fast and was quick in other ways. My coach told the team once I was the best freshman second baseman he ever had. "It's the varsity for Todd next year," he said.

I had spent last summer on my grandpa's farm. Although he lived five miles outside East Powell, I went home only three times. After finishing my work, I'd lie around daydreaming about how strong I'd be by fall and how Kelly and I would finally get together. Now things seemed hopeless.

I stared at the winter sky, wishing baseball season were two weeks instead of four months away. I wanted to feel important again. I wanted people to notice me and say I was still the best. I wanted Kelly.

Chapter
4

The day after the corn incident I went to the lunchroom before serving time, as usual, to eat my portion of slop. I always sat with Diane Gitzke because she was one of those quiet, unassuming girls who was too nice to tease. She smiled and listened, and I ate without worrying about what to say next.

While I ate, I made up my mind that hatred was beneath me. If I stayed clear of Robbie and—yes—Kelly, too, I could proceed with my life and concentrate on studies and, later, baseball. And there was the basketball team.

I was manager. In most schools team managers are students who aren't particularly athletic but who enjoy hanging around the jocks. At East things were different. The managers had a lot of responsibility and at the season's end were honored as highly as the players. I kept track of equipment and everything else that eluded

Coach Smith. People agreed he was a tough trainer who demanded top performances from his boys, but in practical matters he was spaced out. I had plenty to keep me busy.

I was close to polishing off a mealy cherry cobbler when Robbie brought his tray over and sat down. "I got a job washing dishes in here," he said with a big smile. "You're Diane, aren't you? We have art together, right?"

Diane almost gagged attempting to swallow her food and return the smile.

Robbie looked at me. "When I saw you working in here yesterday, it seemed like a good idea, so I applied. Mrs. Chaffhead or Chatney, or whatever her name is, said I lucked out because this guy quit and they needed someone right away. So here I am."

Great.

Diane bent toward Robbie like some lovesick homing pigeon.

"Hope I don't get dishpan hands," he said, examining his large fingers. "I did some dishwashing back in Chicago, and you should have seen the cracks in my skin. Nothing would have helped them. See? I still have scars." Diane murmured sympathetically and practically stuck her face into his palms.

He stabbed at his food. "This stuff's pretty good," he said. I think Diane would have spoon-fed it to him if he had wanted her to. She seemed fascinated by the way he chewed.

"You *like* the food?" I asked.

"Beats eating nothing," he said.

I got up and removed my tray. "Don't rush off," Robbie said. "I want to talk to you." He shoved a cookie into his mouth. "It's algebra."

"What about it?"

"I need help. I'm flunking it. Kelly says you're a straight-A student. That must include algebra."

"What if it does?"

"Are all brains as talkative as you?" He resumed eating.

"Yeah, Todd," Diane said. "What's your problem? You always talk a blue streak."

"I have to get to work," I said, leaving the table.

Maybe if Robbie hadn't come on strong. Maybe if Diane hadn't been so smitten, practically drooling into her food, acting as if her Prince Charming had arrived. I felt protective toward my serving buddy. Girls like Diane never had a chance with guys like Robbie. I knew his game. He only went for the beautiful ones like Kelly, more so if someone else already had them.

I took a good look at him from the counter. He must possess a quality seen only by females—like when you put on 3-D glasses. What that quality was beat me. Then I decided his hair was at least eighty percent of it.

Because of the family baldness curse, my obsession with hair involved every human being I came within fifty yards of. Robbie not only had black curly hair, but it lay back from his face in little waves, matching two thick dark eyebrows. Rather prominent nose. Mouth too large in more ways than one. Couldn't see his teeth. Nope, it had to be the hair. Slender build, but who'd want his skinny body?

Cool it, Richardson. Save your horsepower. He's not worth the sweat.

Grabbing my apron, I slipped the loop over my head and glanced at the utensils, trays and plates to make sure there were plenty of each, another exciting facet of my job. My destiny today? Dishing carrots. Ugh, the whole bin smelled like Lysol.

"I'm serious about what I said." Robbie wore an identical apron and rubber gloves that were short on his hands. "You know, about algebra."

What a persistent kid. "So you're flunking. What do you want me to do?"

"Help me." The guy had phenomenal nerve. "I don't make much money, but I'll pay you what I can. I've got to pass so I can play baseball."

The word "baseball" bounced off my eardrums and slammed into the back of my brain. "Baseball?" I said carefully.

"Yeah, you know." He made batting and catching gestures.

"Baseball," I repeated. "I play baseball."

"Really? Hey, that's great." He started bouncing around.

"You're going to wear yourself out. Practice doesn't start until April first." I crossed my arms against my chest. "What position do you play?" I asked, knowing exactly what the answer would be.

"Second base."

Of course. What else? I wished the carrots would quit stinking. "I play second base," I said. "I've played second base for seven years."

"How about that? Too bad you'll be collecting splinters this year." He grinned. "I'm a little rusty, though. Need some practice. Maybe we could help each other. Well, will you?"

"Will I what?"

"Teach me algebra." He couldn't keep his feet still. They shifted back and forth, taking his body with them as an afterthought. No wonder he was thin. He never relaxed.

"I don't have time," I said. "I manage the basketball team. You might have seen me at the games. And I have plenty of homework at night."

"Do you actually study?"

"Of course. Don't you?"

"Never. I'm a TV addict. I need another job, though. Know of anything?"

I had heard the man at A & L was looking for a clean-up boy. "No," I said. What was the matter with me?

Diane came up to us, not acting like Diane at all. She reminded me of a Pinto trying to be a Corvette. "Time to get going, guys," she said, her voice husky.

"Will you think about it?" Robbie asked me, starting for the dish room.

"Maybe," I said. That was my fatal mistake.

Diane sighed. "He's handsome."

I turned around and glanced into the kitchen. Robbie

was getting the washing machine ready. He saw me and waved.

"Isn't he good-looking?"

"I suppose so."

Diane shoved a serving spoon at me. "What's wrong with him?"

"Wrong?"

"Why don't you like Robbie?"

"I said he looked all right. Does that mean I don't like him?"

"You frowned when you said it."

I stabbed at the carrots. "Maybe it's this job. I can think of ten things I'd rather be doing. Always puts me in a bad mood. I don't know why my dad insists that I keep with it. He makes plenty, but I still have to work for my spending money."

"Guess he wants you to learn. He cares about your future."

"Sure." If he cared, I thought, he'd stay home more, talk to his wife and kid once in a while.

A strange, off-key voice, punctuated by rattling silverware, jarred my thoughts. ". . . Can't you see . . . you're the one for me . . ."

"What in the world is that?" I asked.

Diane giggled. "That's Robbie singing," she said. "At least someone around here's in good spirits."

That night Pete came around and drove me to the bowling alley for some hot chocolate. I felt like a baby being hauled to the kiddie rides at the carnival. I had been dragging for the last few days, and tonight's dinner sat in my stomach like a lump of lard.

After ordering himself a pitcher of beer, Pete said, "Something's bothering you. So what is it, that girl again?" He took a huge swallow. Foam stuck to his mustache. "You ought to like a bunch of them the way I do."

I hadn't even thought of Kelly tonight. More than anything I wanted to go to bed. I was dead tired. "I'm thinking about tutoring this guy in my algebra class," I said, "but maybe I don't want to do it."

"The only thing I can do with my head is stick it under a hood," Pete said, "and look at you. Sounds great to me."

"It's not that great. He has to pass to play baseball, that's all."

"He any good? You need someone decent on that team besides you and Rick."

"He can't be as good as me. Anyway, why should I help him?"

"Is there something wrong with the guy?"

"It doesn't matter," I said. My throat hurt. When had that happened? I took a huge gulp of hot chocolate and choked like mad. "Pete, I have to get home," I said. "I feel lousy." Pete paid and we went out to the truck.

"Guess this must be your bad year, huh?" he said as we drove home. "Everybody's got to have one."

When Pete left me off, I went to my room and flopped on the bed, wondering if I had the energy left to undress and burrow between the covers. Then I remembered the English paper due in the morning. Staggering to my desk, I sifted through notebooks and papers, looking for the rough draft. My throat hurt horribly now. I got out some blank paper, put a tape in my deck and flipped the switch.

"Turn that noise down!" My music always miraculously produced my dad. I heard his heavy steps outside my door. He came in, looking like a flabby balloon, although he was supposed to be dieting.

"Sorry," I said, trying to smile, "I wasn't thinking."

"You do have earphones."

I saw how tired he looked. The creases that started on the outsides of his eyes curved down his face, and under his eyelids the bags were bluer than his irises.

"Do you want to sit down or something?" I asked.

He went to my bed and lowered himself with a sigh. "What are you doing?"

"Just copying over a paper," I said. "It's pretty bad."

"You're doing all right, aren't you?"

"In school? Sure, I guess." When is he going to have the operation? I wondered. He looks terrible. I swallowed. The pain was worse. "Were you—" He crossed one leg over the other. Married men didn't look strange doing that. "Did you have to work hard in school like I do?"

Dad seemed amused. "My grades were atrocious," he said. "I didn't care about anything but sports, which got me nowhere."

I didn't entirely believe him, since he was a type A who cared and worried about everything. "But sports does a lot for you," I said, "like—"

"Oh, let's not get into that," he said. Great. My dad didn't even have time to let me finish a sentence. "What

I mean is . . ." He looked around as if searching for a word. "It's all right to have fun playing games—up to a point—but life isn't that kind of game. It's hard—working and giving your family what it wants and needs."

What I want, I thought, is for you to slow down. You don't owe me *things*. When I get married I'll keep myself healthy and spend time with my kids. That's what I'll give them.

"When I was your age I thought the world was my oyster and I was the pearl. But . . ."

But what?

He struggled to get up, his eyes looking past me. "Guess I'll hit the hay," he said. "Keep the volume down."

"Sure," I said.

I lay in bed that night thinking of the Sunday afternoons Dad and I used to lie around and watch football, running outside at halftime to play a little catch in the yard. What had happened to days like that? Days of taking Mom to her favorite restaurant, hamming it up, acting like her knights in shining armor. Days of kidding around with Grandpa when Dad and I visited him on a boiling summer afternoon and sat at his kitchen table discussing politics over lemonade. When the conversation got hot and heavy, both of them would burst out laughing, and I would, too.

Dad didn't go out there at all now. He had no interest in his family. All he wanted to do was work. I hardly ever saw him anymore. When had this happened?

And when, exactly, had we stopped talking to each other?

Chapter
5

The next morning I went to school despite my sore throat and fell asleep in two of my classes. Not just nodding off, but head-on-the-desk, heavy-breathing sleep, complete with loud snoring, as both morning teachers later testified.

"Go home," Mrs. Rangone said, hauling me to my feet after class. "You have a serious concentration block." I staggered to the cafeteria to tell Mrs. Chaffey that serving was out today. When I got there, I sat down and conked out again. Diane woke me up once. Then I heard another familiar voice.

"What's wrong with you?"

I lifted my head and tried focusing through a feverish haze. All I saw were Robbie's black eyes.

"Are you sick?"

"I think so."

"What's the matter with your voice?"

"My throat is killing me."

"Well, what are you doing here, trying to infect everybody?"

"I'm going home," I assured him, "as soon as I take a nap."

"Come on," he said, pulling at my arm, "I'll take you to the nurse."

"I know how to get there. Leave me alone." Even now I don't understand why Robbie bothered with me at all.

"Diane," I heard him say, "Todd's sick. Tell Randall to get over here and help me. I'll make sure he doesn't fall out of his chair."

I didn't really wake up until Dr. Golden gave me a blood test in his office. I found out later I had mononucleosis and strep. I didn't care. I wanted to sleep for a year.

Christmas and New Year's slipped by. Once when I got up to go to the bathroom I glanced in the mirror and scared myself. What had happened to my eyes? They were all wrinkled. Would I always look like this? I had a bad case, and even when I became more wakeful, Dr. Golden said I hadn't improved much.

Rick came to see me three weeks after I took to my bed. "You look terrible," he said. "You must have lost ten pounds."

"At least. How is everyone?" Meaning Kelly, of course.

"Nothing's changed. We've been having some good workouts after school. We won our last two games, one in overtime."

"I know. What are you doing for a manager? I shouldn't be in this cave much longer."

He bit his fingernail. "Got a new one. Had to. You know Coach Smith. If his head wasn't attached, he wouldn't be able to find it. Kelly's coming over to see you one of these days, so fix yourself up or you'll shock her. When are you coming back, anyway?"

"Might be another month. What a drag."

"What did the doctor say about baseball?"

"That I might not get to play. But he's wrong. If I can't play baseball, I'm going to kill myself."

"Sure you are. First things first, old buddy. You have other years."

"I have my reasons for playing this year." The picture of Samson scooping up a fast grounder gave me a momentary surge of adrenaline. "I'm second baseman this year, and that's history," I said. "By the way, how's your shooting?"

"I've been averaging twenty-two points a game," Rick said.

"You're kidding. That much?"

Rick shrugged. Others should be so modest. "Do you know who plays good ball? Robbie. We've been messing around, playing one-on-one during free period. I can't figure out why he never went out. He's good, Todd."

My stomach felt funny. "Why bring him up? I'm not interested in anything he does." I thought of how he would play. Admittedly, he had the right stretched-out look.

"You seemed interested enough when what he did involved Kelly."

"Is he . . . are they . . . say no more. If he's anywhere near her, he's after anything he can get."

"What's wrong with him? He's an all-right guy. Remember Deuter?"

"I haven't been gone that long, Rick."

"You know how left-footed he is and how bad he wants to be one of us. Not that I blame him. Well, Robbie takes him aside one day and says, 'Deuter, the ball is not meant to be handled in the manner you have been handling it. I would like to show you Samson's surefire method of success.'"

"You're making tears come to my eyes—"

"No, hold on. So Robbie helps the kid. Everyone knows Deuter is hopeless. To be honest, he always got in my way."

"So, what does that prove?"

"Deuter's still hopeless. Let's face it, you can't make a fudge brownie out of a piece of mud. But Robbie made Deuter feel like he was—well, you know, wanted. Now we're all nice to Deuter. Actually, the kid isn't all that bad."

"Why isn't Robbie on the team if he's so good?"

"I guess he must be ineligible because of his grades."

"That I don't doubt." I looked at the floor.

"Old buddy, you have a one-track mind about him. Robbie tries pretty hard to get along. I like him. Sorry."

"That's your privilege. Can we change the subject?"

After Rick left I lay there, frustrated and depressed. Any exertion and my body became Jell-O. I wanted to will myself well. I had to get back with my friends before I turned loony. But mono takes its time.

One afternoon the phone rang. "It's me, the dish room

delight," Robbie said. "I need help with my math, like immediately."

"You woke me up."

"What are you doing asleep?"

"I can't help it. I've been put to sleep by the bad fairy, and I'm waiting for my lover to wake me up with a kiss."

"Sorry, I'm booked up. When can I come over?"

"Did I ever say I'd tutor you? Anyway, you can't come. I'm not supposed to do my own schoolwork yet."

"You can't get ready for baseball by laying around all the time."

"Maybe I won't get to play. That wouldn't disappoint you, would it, Samson, since I'm your competition for second base."

Robbie laughed. "What competition? Maybe you better not go out. I'd hate to see you cry."

"We'll see who bawls when the cuts are made."

"Just remember to take defeat like a man."

I hung up on him.

Rick brought me homework assignments the next week. I knew Kelly would show up eventually, but how could she while my eyes were still screwy and my ribs stuck out? My skin looked watery, too, making the freckles lose their zip. The freckle part was okay.

When she called I got jittery. She wanted to bring other friends, but I told her the rule was one visitor at a time. After showering, I put on after-shave and tried to get my hair into some kind of shape. I didn't want her to see my pajamas, so I got dressed and lay down again to wait for her, pulling the covers over me.

"Todd." Damn, I had gone to sleep. I felt my mouth. Had I drooled? "Your front door was unlocked." Kelly set a plate on my desk.

"What's that?" I asked, pointing.

"Cookies from my mother."

"Tell her thanks." She walked over to me, looking so good I forgot I was fully dressed and still under the covers.

"Are you contagious?" she asked, showing me two gorgeous dimples.

I swallowed, my tongue shriveled and dry. "I guess not by now."

"Then I'll sit by you."

I nodded. She sat on the bed at about my waist and put her hand on my arm. The resulting sensation told me my body wasn't dying after all. I always reacted in the same way around Kelly—all nervous. Now here she was, close enough in her white sweater to touch. Pretty face. Hair that never stayed where she combed it, soft like her eyes. When she smiled, her eye teeth overlapped the next teeth forward, and she had the habit of licking her lips and running a finger over her teeth—to check for lipstick, maybe.

"You look different," she said, softly.

"Yeah, I know. I'm a mess."

"No, that isn't what I mean." She tilted her head and raised her hand to my face. "You look older. Your cheekbones show. It makes you quite handsome."

My face flushed. "Really?"

"Before, your face was round, and now just look at

your nose." I crossed my eyes. "It's even better, and your chin is more prominent. I definitely think you should try to stay at this weight." She gave me a devilish grin. "Sure you're not contagious?"

"I hope not."

"I'll take my chances. This is from me and all the girls at East." She bent toward me and I smelled some scented soap and she kissed my cheek. I couldn't help it—my brute instinct got the best of me. I turned my head, wrapped my arms around her and kissed her in one motion. At first I thought she'd push me away, but she held my head against her chest and stroked my hair.

"Poor Todd," she said.

"I've missed you," I whispered. "Let's be together again."

She shook her head, stood up and rearranged herself while I tried to become unexcited, glad to be under the covers after all but hurt by the way she'd cut me off, just about the same way my mother chopped apart chickens.

"Let's talk some more," she said.

"Okay." I tried to stop staring at the breasts I had just felt beneath that white sweater by fixing my eyes on the wall. "I wish I was out of here," I said. "It's like the night of the living dead."

"You're missed," she said. "There's no one in Nash's class to answer questions anymore. And this is important: I wanted to ask you if you're going to be able to help Robbie with his math now that you're better. He's barely slipping by. I've tried, but you have a better understanding."

Why was it his name came up in every conversation I had with anyone? Was he the only kid at East, for crying out loud?

"He's a very good friend, Todd."

"Not of mine." The urge to bite down on something made me disentangle myself from the covers and go for a cookie. "Want one?" She shook her head.

"You don't like him," she said. "He's one of the nicest boys I've ever met."

That's the whole point. "So I've been told. Several times. You should have seen the job he did on Diane."

"Diane Gitzke?"

"She almost fell into her soup with ecstasy the first time she met him."

"Robbie wouldn't give a girl the wrong idea. When you get to know him—"

"I have no intention of doing that." *Don't jam him down my throat.*

"Just do this one thing for me." She walked to me and started to put out her hand, then stopped. "Look at it this way. He needs your help and you have all this ability. Forget how you feel for a while. I mean, lots of teachers don't like certain students, but they at least tolerate them."

"I don't know."

"It won't hurt you to help him."

I remained silent. Kelly lifted her chin. "I'm going to tell you something, Todd Richardson. Someday you and Robbie are going to be friends."

I stared at her as if she were crazy. Robbie had everyone wrapped around his little finger. Was I missing something somewhere?

"Very good friends," she said, pulling on her coat. "You wait. It's going to happen."

"Never," I said after she left. I chomped down on another cookie. "I'll never forgive him for taking you away from me."

Chapter
6

The Monday before I went back to school Mom announced that my grandpa was moving in with us for a while. I was surprised because he always said he'd never leave his farm. That was when Mom finally let me in on Dad's bypass. Grandpa wanted to be around to help, she said.

When Pete found out, he was upset. "Can I do something?" he asked. "I didn't know he was so sick. Why didn't you tell me?" I had to admit I had no more information than he did.

I worried Dad might die. Should I say something to him, like I'm glad I'm your son? Thanks for working your butt off for us, but look where it got you? Who will take care of Mom?

As a little kid I used to get all excited waiting for Grandpa to arrive. He swore and snored like a beast. He was such fun! I don't think Mom understood him, but she admired the way he kept the farm, though she didn't approve of his personal habits. I couldn't believe her expression every time he belched.

He moved into the attic instead of the second-floor guest room. The attic room was bigger and Grandpa thought running up and down the stairs was good for him. If my dad had farmed instead of beating his head against the wall of his agency, he might have been healthy like Grandpa.

Grandpa sold his livestock, saying that February was a good time to move, since it was dull out there away from everybody. I knew he was lying. He drove in for a visit anytime he wanted, and being alone had never bothered him. He wanted Mom to feel secure. He was that way, and when he arrived she threw her arms around his stocky body as though she never wanted to let go. The whole scene made me uncomfortable, but I was still glad to see him.

He and I had our usual arm-wrestling competition, and, of course, he won.

"Wait, Grandpa," I warned. "Someday you're going down." He laughed.

He spent the first few days driving around in his Porsche, getting supplies for his new room, building himself a bookcase and visiting all the neighbors to let them know he had arrived and was ready to socialize.

One afternoon while he went downtown, I sat in front of the TV watching a repeat of "Gilligan's Island," fantasizing about Kelly and making a respectable throw with a pillow to third base, the green chair in the corner.

I was eating continuously out of boredom, wishing Grandpa were back. We had a blackjack series going and I was leading so far. We played for pennies. I especially liked it when he dealt double-downs and I could bet on two cards at once.

I heard someone at the front door, and, thinking it was either Grandpa or Pete, I went and opened it, my eyes still fixed on the TV screen. I turned to see Robbie Samson standing there. He was wearing an ugly plaid jacket.

"What do you want?" I asked.

"I brought my algebra book," he said. "I know you're better now. Rick told me."

"It's been six weeks. Haven't you flunked yet?"

He laughed. "Not yet. Still hanging by an eyelash. It doesn't look like you're doing anything anyway. I said I'd pay."

"I don't want your money." I saw Grandpa drive up and hop out of his Porsche. "I've decided not to tutor you, so why don't you—"

"I found one!" Grandpa yelled, waving a small bag.

Robbie turned. "Who's that?" he asked, a slow grin creeping over his face.

"My grandpa. He lives with us."

Grandpa hurried up the steps and stopped when he got to Robbie and me. "How do," he said, shoving a big hand at Robbie. They shook hands. Grandpa put some pressure into that one. "My name's Buck Richardson. What's yours?"

"Robbie Samson."

"Well, come on in. Let's keep the oil bill down and

close the door." He turned to me. "I found the right hook for that plant hanger your mother wants, and I'll get it up before she comes home. I knew it'd be somewhere in this town, and I nearly tore the place apart trying to find it. Say—" He looked at Robbie. "Would you like to see my room? I have a paradise in the attic, and I can smoke up there since Todd's mom is one of those allergic little things. There's a vent that goes right to the outside. Come on, Todd, let's show Robbie."

"I don't think he—" I began. I had to get rid of him before Grandpa got the wrong idea.

"This way," Grandpa said, waving his arms around like an energetic bird. "Robbie you say your name is? I don't remember you from the last time I was here, but I'd take to any friend of Todd. I've always liked Todd's pals—Rick, Walt, all of them. Are you a buddy from the team or from a particular class or—"

"We aren't too well acquainted yet. Todd's helping me with math." I tried to give him a dirty look, but he wasn't facing me. "We moved here last August from Chicago," Robbie continued. "My dad doesn't like big cities. He needed a change and someone told him East Powell was all right, so here we are."

"So you're a family of two, are you?"

Robbie nodded and stood stiffly beside Grandpa until Grandpa put his hand on Robbie's shoulder. Immediately Robbie relaxed. He'd found a friend.

"Come upstairs now and see my room. I can cuss all I want up there and who's to care?" Robbie laughed and Grandpa punched him.

"Excuse me," I said, "I thought you came to—" But

they had already reached the first landing. I followed them up part of the way, noticing how knock-kneed Robbie was. I went back down.

"Todd?" Grandpa hollered. I pretended not to hear, but after a few minutes of wondering what was going on, I went up.

"You'd dress it up with a few interesting posters, huh?" Grandpa was asking.

"Yeah, a couple of girls to keep you company. Everything's so—"

"Vapid?" I offered, standing in the doorway.

"Exactly," Robbie said. "Whatever that means."

"Colorless, dull, uninteresting, boring, lifeless."

Grandpa snickered. "Well then, I'll have to get me some. Where would one buy such a poster?"

"I got mine at Simmon's Cigar Shop."

"Grandpa doesn't need stuff like that." I glared at Robbie, who was fiddling with a little figurine.

"My mom had one of these," he said, putting it down carefully. "I don't know how my dad got it, but I broke it. Talk about pissed off."

"That's the only one left. Over a thirty-year period I somehow broke every damn thing my wife held dear," Grandpa said. "She called me a goat at a tea party. I was forever apologizing, but that didn't stop the tears. She never got resentful, though. That's what I loved about old Phyllis."

"I only ruined one thing," Robbie said, "but that was enough. I made sure I kept hands off after that." He looked down at the piece of china, then over at Grandpa.

"Your room is great," he said, grinning. "I'd give anything to have one like it."

"I know," Grandpa said. "It's my Shangri-La." He looked at me. "So what's going on in the lives of handsome young men these days?"

Robbie glanced in my direction. "Well," he said, "since there's only one fitting that description in this room, let me just mention a few statistics. If I had to rate the parts of my life, I'd say that sports is ninety percent important, girls are eighty-five percent important and schoolwork falls somewhere around five percent."

"That's a hundred and eighty percent, Samson. You need math lessons, all right—elementary math."

"We all have special abilities," Grandpa said, "as well as certain, well, deficiencies. In my case I could never, for the life of me, carry a tune."

"Really?" Robbie almost danced. "Man, neither can I."

"Doesn't surprise me."

"My whole life I'd had a hidden desire to croon like Bing Crosby, but the only living things that appreciate my singing are my cows, bless their hearts. They join right in, and I have to admit we all sound alike."

"Yeah, I know what you mean. I'm out with a bunch of guys and I think I'm doing great, really ripping the scales, and then—"

"Someone has to tell you you couldn't sing your way out of a paper bag," Grandpa said.

"Right." They both laughed.

I turned my head and looked out the window. All I

saw were bare branches, but it was better than looking at Samson.

"I think I'll put that hanger up now before your mother gets home, Todd," Grandpa said. "Why don't you two go down and grab yourselves some brain food before you start your lesson?"

"I think I'll need some," Robbie said.

"Good meeting you, Robbie. You come back and see me, okay?"

Robbie looked at me, then back at Grandpa. "Okay," he said softly.

We went down to the den. Robbie gazed around the room. "This is nice," he said. "I like your house."

"It's just a house."

"I never had anything like this." He shifted around, examining everything in the room. I wondered if he'd ever settle down. "Are you going to help me?" he said finally. "I swear I'll pay you."

"You had to tell Grandpa I was going to, didn't you?"

"I was just giving him a reason I knew you."

"Yeah, sure. Well, now I'll have to do it."

"I don't think it's going to kill you. All I need is an hour a day."

"You don't have to beg."

"Why don't we go up to your room?"

"This place is fine." He wasn't getting one foot into my territory. "Fill me in on what you need to know and I'll try to do something today. Get your book."

He obeyed. I motioned him to the game table. "Start talking," I ordered when we sat down.

"Your grandpa sure is nice."

I gave him a look. "Not about my grandpa—algebra."

"Oh." He opened his book. "I need help with everything. I'm way behind."

"Can I ask you a question? Are you dumb or just lazy?"

Robbie leaned back on two chair legs. My mother never allowed that. "If I wanted to, I could make As in algebra and everything else."

"Then why don't you?"

He shrugged. "I don't care about school, only baseball, and I have to pass to play. I can't charm Nash, but all my other teachers are women, and when I tell them how pretty they look, they let me by."

I believed that. "You practice on Diane, too, don't you?"

"What do you mean?"

"She called me the other night and told me you were going to the Backwards Dance with her."

"With Diane?" He looked confused. Another act. He sat up. "Diane didn't ask me."

"I don't buy it."

"She didn't. I swear it. Kelly asked me. She and I are going."

That was worse. Ever since Diane told me Robbie was taking her, I had the wild delusion Kelly might ask me. My throat felt like baked dirt. Taking a monstrous breath, I calmed myself. One of you is lying, and I vote for you, Samson, I thought. "Let's start," I said, pointing to his book.

"Man, I mean it. I don't know what you're talking about. Did she really say we were going? Diane?" He stared at me with his black eyes.

"Let's drop it."

Robbie nodded. "Yeah, later. I've got to get to basketball practice soon."

I leaned toward him. *What?* "Since when are you on the team?"

"I'm not on the team." He spoke slowly. "I'm the manager now."

I stood up so fast the chair crashed to the floor behind me. "That's my job!" I yelled. "Is there anything else I should know?"

"Didn't you hear I was manager?" He was blushing. "You couldn't do it while you were sick, right?"

"Right, but . . ."

"Someone had to. I don't see what the big deal is."

"Why you?"

"Why not me? Rick and the rest of the team asked me to do it."

"So Rick told you to go for it."

Robbie got up, closing his book. "I'll leave now," he said. "You'd rather teach your worst enemy. Or is that what I am?"

I didn't answer. I left the room. When I went back in, he had gone.

Chapter
7

I called him that night after dinner. I don't know what it was, but as much as he irked me, he did have a point. He *was* going to pay me to tutor him, and someone had to manage the team. I figured one call wouldn't kill me.

I heard a sharp, low hello. I knew he had a dad, but the voice surprised me.

"Is Robbie there?" I asked. The man didn't answer but called to him.

"Yeah?" Robbie said.

"This is Todd. Look," I mumbled, "I suppose I might have said that I'd help you, so I will. Come over tomorrow night. We'll do algebra, nothing else—no talking, only business." I felt like a moron.

"It'll have to be after school. I work nights." His voice was flat.

"After school," I repeated and hung up.

"There's a guy coming over tomorrow because I'm

helping him with math," I told Mom at dinner. "It's a business deal." My dad seemed mildly interested. He had come home in time for dinner but didn't appear to be eating.

"I hope you won't be late," Mom said.

"He's coming in the afternoon for an hour. That's about all I can stand of him."

Grandpa's eyebrows rose an inch.

"Todd," my mother said with *that* edge to her voice. If Samson came to the door when she was home, he'd get the Anne Richardson therapy: a boost to the ego, a small but meaningful touch on the shoulder and concerned eye contact. Knowing Robbie's tactics, I could see him maneuvering himself into my mother's graces, then hanging around while she crammed him full of brownies.

The next afternoon Robbie arrived at three-thirty with some rolled-up papers under his arm. "Is your grandpa here?" he asked, throwing his jacket down. "I've got something for him. Look." He undid two posters, one at a time, revealing two curvy beauties with next to nothing on. They were hand-drawn. I could see the smudge marks. "What do you think?"

"My mother will have a fit if she ever sees them," I answered. "Grandpa's in his room. Where did they come from?"

"I drew them." He ran upstairs with his gifts. I sneaked up after him.

"What a nice thing for you to do," I heard Grandpa say. "Thank you very much, Robbie. They're beautiful."

I sighed and went back down. A few minutes later Robbie returned.

"Where did you learn to draw like that?" I asked.

"I don't know. I've always done it."

"Well, you're good."

"Thanks a lot." He smiled at me. I looked away. "Anyway, before we start I want to settle the money thing," Robbie said. "What are you going to charge me? It shouldn't be too much, since you don't have any experience. How's five dollars—or do you want more?"

"It depends on how well you learn," I said.

We sat down and I began his lesson. I couldn't believe his lack of knowledge of the most elementary principles. "What have you been all year in class, comatose?" I asked after fifteen minutes of zero progress.

"I mainly daydream," he said, "or look at boobs."

"How has Mr. Nash been able to grade you when you know absolutely nothing?"

"I copy someone else's papers."

That afternoon I attempted to take Robbie through positive integers and monomials, but the more I talked, the jumpier he got. An hour had passed and I was getting nowhere with him.

"Don't you remember anything?" I asked. He shook his head. "Well, concentrate then, so it doesn't take the rest of the school year to get through the first ten pages."

"I have to go to practice," he said suddenly. "When should I come again?"

"Monday. Read these two chapters and work the problems at the end."

"Okay, Professor," he said. "Guess I'm not ready to take the world apart—in math, that is. But the girls don't care about that, do they?" he added with a grin. "Especially when they look at my body."

"How did your teaching go?" Mom asked later.

"Opposite poles repel," I said. "When's Dad going to the hospital?"

"Dr. Golden's trying to schedule surgery for the fifth," she said. "Your father's going in for tests in about a week. Just don't worry too much. Everything's going to be fine."

If everything was going to be so fine, why did Mom look like a wreck whenever I brought Dad up, and why did this picture of Dad dying keep slipping in and out of my mind like someone playing hide-and-seek?

Chapter
8

Back in school I inhaled the familiar old musty smell that permeated the halls and rooms, and I had the odd sensation that life had gone on without me. The last game of the basketball season was a week from Friday. Dr. Golden had scheduled my dad's bypass two weeks after that.

By the end of my first day back I was exhausted. I caught sight of Kelly once when she and Robbie crossed the campus after third period. He had his arm around her. I thought of following them.

I felt a nudge. "I'm glad you're back." Diane stood next to me. "You went running off after English, so I couldn't talk to you. Are you ever pale!"

"Yeah, I know." I wanted to ask her about the dance Friday, but I decided it wouldn't be right. Who would want to be reminded that she'd been thrown over for somebody better-looking? "How've you been?" I asked.

"Better. But I shouldn't complain after all you've been through." She sighed and patted my arm. "You should go home," she said. "You look bad."

"I guess so, since Samson's coming over for his algebra lesson."

At the mention of his name I saw a light go out in Diane's eyes. It made me want to find Samson and punch him.

"He didn't take me to the dance after all. Did you hear? Kelly asked him, too, and well, I got sick and called it off, and then—"

"You don't have to lie," I said. "I know exactly what happened."

Diane blushed. "You do? But how could you?"

"I think it's rotten." Diane looked as if she would cry. "But don't worry. You've learned a lesson, and maybe now you'll give up on him."

Diane made a face and edged away from me. "Yes, well—guess I'll see you tomorrow."

Diane's reaction confused me. Now at least she knew what kind of treatment Robbie dealt out. If only she were a ravishing beauty, so he would go for her and leave Kelly for me.

When I got home, Robbie was already sitting in the den with Grandpa, who got up and motioned me to his chair. "Your skin looks like milk," he commented. "Robbie's been telling me about Chicago. I used to get down there when your grandma was alive."

"Did you do the problems and the reading?" I asked Robbie.

"I didn't have much time over the weekend," he said. I could imagine.

During his lesson Robbie again was preoccupied. More than once he shifted around, got up and sat again. "I can't teach you if you aren't going to listen to me," I said. "What's wrong with you? Can't you sit still?"

"Sorry," he said. "I guess I should get to practice now. Give me the assignment for tomorrow." He looked up at me from where he slumped. "You still think I dumped Diane, don't you?"

"Shut up about Diane," I answered. "And if you don't do any better on the math, I'm through helping you."

"All right," he sighed, "I'll try." He got up and left.

He came over every afternoon that week. As quiet as he had been at first, I was almost able to tolerate him, but then he changed, reemerging as a high-geared joker, yakking with Grandpa and discussing sports with Pete when he stopped over on Wednesday. After his previous sessions, which had been real disasters, he surprised me by absorbing algebra with amazing speed, finishing every assignment I gave him. I was disappointed. I had expected him to fail.

One afternoon Robbie stayed and went upstairs with Grandpa after his lesson.

"Come on, Richardson," Robbie said.

"Todd, bring us up something to eat while you're at it."

Great. I scrounged together some cookies, tea, milk and carrot sticks, and watched Robbie eat and drink almost everything after I had carried the tray upstairs.

"You're lucky," he said as he downed the last bit of milk, "to have someone fixing you stuff like this. Got anything else you don't want—to eat, I mean?"

"Tell you what," Grandpa said. "When you're ready to go, I'll fix you up a care package. Annie always makes too much, and if it weren't for my running up and down the stairs, I'd be putting on an awful lot of fat. See, at my farm there's a heap of hard work, but it keeps me healthy. Todd's dad used to be healthy—happy, too, if my memory serves me." Grandpa's face changed expression.

"I'm sorry about Mr. Richardson," Robbie said, then looked at me. "I bet you worry about your dad a lot."

"How did you know? Did you tell him, Grandpa?"

"It's been on my mind, and I always have to talk about what's on my mind."

"He'll be okay," Robbie said.

"Don't say something empty and stupid like that," I told him as I went to the door. "How do you know, anyway?"

Robbie shrugged. "I guess when it comes to dads, you always hope," he said.

As the days passed I saw how much Grandpa anticipated Robbie's visits. I hardly got to talk to my own grandfather, and I wasn't going to try while Robbie made a pest of himself. Why couldn't I tell him to get out of my house and my life? Something made me keep quiet. Maybe the thought that the more he came to our place, the less he'd be with Kelly.

I hadn't talked to her more than twice that week. All

she did was thank me for helping Robbie, which I had come to regret. She seemed to talk to me out of obligation now. Every night I went to bed angry, wondering what was wrong with me to have become such a nothing in her eyes. It was as if our time together had never been.

One afternoon Robbie came bounding down the stairs. "Your grandpa's a wild man," he said. "I wish I had a grandpa." He plopped on the couch.

"You act like you do," I said from my chair. Just then my mom and dad came through the front door. Robbie leaped up. "What's the matter?" I asked.

"Your parents—I didn't know they'd be here."

"My parents happen to live here," I said. "This is their house."

"I'd better go," he said, looking like a trapped animal.

"Man, you're strange."

"I get nervous around some people. What if they don't like me?"

A wise choice on their part, I thought. "You don't have any trouble with Grandpa," I said, "and what about all the teachers you say you charm?"

"I don't know. I can't explain it."

"You might as well meet them. My mom will bawl me out if I don't introduce you."

My mother walked over, holding out her hand to Robbie. "You must be Todd's friend," she said, taking his big hand in both her little ones. Robbie gave her a shy smile. My dad shook his hand briefly.

"You're Robbie?" he asked. Robbie nodded, now

mute. He was beginning to remind me of a chameleon, changing colors depending upon who occupied his space.

"Robbie, would you like to have dinner with us? I'm not planning much, but you're welcome to stay," my mother said.

"He can't," I said.

Mom gave me a pointed look while Dad went to hang up their coats.

Grandpa came in. "Call your father," he said in his loud voice. "It'll be a pleasure to have you stay."

"He's at work. He doesn't get home until eleven."

"Do you always make your own dinner then?" Mom asked.

Oh hell. She's going to invite him to move in.

"I work three nights a week at the Lamplighter, so I eat there." He glanced at me. "Maybe I'd better not stay."

"Hey, don't let me stop you," I said. "In fact, you can take my place at the table, because I've lost my appetite." I made for the stairs, taking them three at a time. I calculated the time it took my mom to get dinner on the table, then realized that Robbie would eat my food if I didn't get back down there.

My mother's great talent was what I call "smoothing." She smoothed out any situation, even if she didn't understand it. Now she simply smiled and passed me a plate as I sat down.

Robbie occupied my seat.

"I was just going up to get you," Mom said in her most

pleasant voice, "and here you are. Have some meat loaf."

"Where?" I asked. There was hardly any left. I examined the bowl that now had five kernels of corn left in it. A shriveled potato sat tiredly on a large platter. "I thought we were having dinner," I said, my voice a little too loud.

My dad frowned at me. "That's enough, Todd," he said, rising. He turned to my mother. "I have some calls to make tonight."

"Fine," she said.

I gave my dad a look. "Does that mean I can't play my stereo?" My room was right over the den.

He crossed his arms against his chest. "Son," he said, "the way I see it, about four of those phone calls paid for that stereo upstairs. One or two got you those fancy shoes you're wearing. Need I say more?"

"I guess not," I mumbled.

Robbie held up one of his legs. His sneaker was falling apart. "Flea-market special," he said.

My dad chuckled as he left the room.

Mom turned to me. "Robbie's been telling us about all the cities he's lived in."

"Like where?" I asked, thinking I might have to settle for a bowl of Raisin Bran.

"Well, let's see." He actually used a napkin on his mouth. "Chicago—you know that—Trenton, Philadelphia, Gary and here. East Powell's best. Hope we stay here."

Sure you do, because of Kelly, you jerk.

"It must be fun seeing so many different places," Mom said.

Robbie smiled faintly. "I never liked moving that much." He stretched. "That was great, Mrs. Richardson. Thanks a lot." He gave my mother a very different sort of look from any I'd seen, one a girl might describe as engaging. To me it was merely repulsive. He always went at females that way in school, too. "I'll help you clean up," he said.

"Heavens, I wouldn't think of having you do anything," Mom said.

Grandpa, who probably enjoyed watching me forage for food, broke the silence that followed. "He gets enough dishes in the cafeteria and the restaurant. He needs spoiling."

"I'd really like to see your room," Robbie said. "Rick says you've got everything, like all the best tapes and a million baseball posters."

"Sorry," I said, "I only take friends up there." I started walking to the stairs.

"Todd," my mother called, and I knew to expect the worst. "I'm rather tired tonight, so you'll have to clean up the dinner dishes for me. Don't forget the pans or the trash." What was she trying to pull? I never had to work in the kitchen.

"Come on, Robbie, I think those pictures I told you about are in my room," Grandpa said, putting his arm around Robbie's shoulders.

Robbie looked at me. Then he winked. You bastard, I thought.

"We'll be upstairs when you finish," Grandpa said to me, dropping his wrinkled napkin on a plate.

When I had finished the last pan and walked into the living room, Robbie had his jacket on. Grandpa's arm still rested on his shoulder. Was it stuck there permanently? Mom stood before Robbie, wearing the smile she gave me when I got sick. Why couldn't either of them see what he was trying to do?

I froze, clenching my fists and teeth at the same time. What could Mom see in Robbie? What did the girls see in him, and, most of all, why had I been dumb enough to let him anywhere near me?

"I think," I said as I reached them, "that you've had enough lessons to pass algebra. You won't need to come here anymore."

One side of Mom's mouth was twitching—I knew she was really angry.

"I guess you're right," Robbie said. "Anyway, I can handle it now. What do I owe you?"

"A pound of flesh," I said.

"You're going to draw my face, don't forget," Grandpa said. "Robbie wants to sketch me—how about that—and me past my prime. Todd here thinks I only have enough time for one grandson, but once a grandpa gets the hang of it, he can be grandpa to anyone he likes, true, Todd?"

Total humiliation. It was the closest my grandfather had ever come to criticizing me.

Mom patted Robbie's arm. "You come again, honey," she said.

"Thanks for dinner, Mrs. Richardson," he said. "I

loved your cooking. It was so nice meeting you." Mom beamed and went to the kitchen. "See you tomorrow," he told me, picking up his book and waving. I didn't move. "Bye, Buck."

Buck? He called my grandpa Buck?

Grandpa and I stood alone in the living room. Here it comes, I thought, but I don't want it. Grandpa understood situations better than you wanted him to. That's why I couldn't fathom his blindness about Robbie.

"Todd, I never tell you what to do. You know that."

Right on schedule. "Sure, Grandpa."

He began to pace, his square body moving slowly around the room. I started walking around the other way.

"Have you ever seen a baby animal that has lost its mother before it's weaned? Or a young animal that's been rejected by its mother and has to find a substitute mother or some such environment? I've watched quite a few of those situations over the years on the farm. It's a pretty simple principle. Find nourishment or die."

Why was he talking about a corny subject like this?

"So what did you do, get up at night and feed them?"

"Sometimes. Remember that bloodhound bitch I had, Peaches? About ten years ago she had a single puppy at the same time my cat Bertha had her litter. Bertha died after her kittens were three days old. You can guess the rest."

"Right. Did you take the kittens to the dog or what?"

"Nope, Peaches found them all by herself and took real good care of them. She was a better mother than Bertha, if the truth be known."

"Did the kittens think they were dogs, or did the pup act like a cat?"

"Those cats knew what they were, but they wouldn't have survived without Peaches. She gave them what they required at the time. When they didn't need her milk anymore, they went off, not especially grateful but alive just the same."

I sank down on the couch. "I thought you were going to talk about Robbie." Grandpa smiled. "Why do you like him so much when he's such a pain?"

"It's easy," Grandpa said. "What strikes me is how hard it would be to hate him."

"He's a fake, a liar and a cheat."

"Those are big words to use on anyone you don't know well. I'm not going to defend him, but the only way to face jealousy is to admit it and start with your insides and work out."

"Jealous? Why? He only wants everything I have and won't stop until he has all of it. I'm getting the raw end of the whole thing."

"Maybe he needs those things more than you."

"He's not getting anything from me except a fight if he keeps it up."

"If Robbie told you some of the things he's told me—"

"Not interested." I tried to reason what baby animals had in common with Robbie. There had to be a connection. "Well," I said, "if you don't have anything more you want to say—"

"Just a minute," Grandpa said. "There is something else. This is my house, too. At least I help with the payments and do my share of the chores. I'd go haywire if I didn't. So certain privileges are mine, like having friends up to my room. Young Rob is my friend, and if you don't like seeing him here, I suggest you leave when he comes to visit me."

"I'll follow your suggestion to the letter," I snapped as I left. My head hurt like crazy, probably because of the fifty calories' worth of food I'd managed to scrounge.

As I passed the den I paused. If only I could talk to my dad, just for a few minutes. But I went on. He wouldn't want to be bothered when he was on the phone.

In my room I put on a tape, turned the volume to low and got into bed, feeling strange and empty.

Chapter
9

At noon on Friday Robbie was surrounded by girls holding up "Beat the Beavers" banners before the pep assembly for the final basketball game. That's how he was at school, charming the women and running around nonstop, but this hotshot act of his couldn't last forever. Sooner or later he had to trip over one of his smooth remarks and flatten his overactive mouth. ·

Kelly walked up to him from around the side of the building, sliding her hand up his arm. He turned and kissed her. The other girls squealed, probably hoping to be next. He cared, really cared for her. His face showed it. Why did he have to care for the only girl I ever loved?

I started for the gym door. A hand grabbed my arm and I turned to look up into Robbie's black eyes. "Going in now?" he asked. "We'll sit with you."

"Get lost," I mumbled, shaking my arm loose.

"Hey," he said, "what's this, my fine algebra teacher?

You should've stayed home last night. I was going to give you some of my secrets for being a magnificent lover. Since you're big on brains and I'm great on charm—"

"Will you just cut the crap?" I said. A flash of what—pain?—crossed his face, but I dismissed it. I had attempted too many times to bury my hate, and the way my stomach churned, I was aching to fight him. But he'd kill me. I had to admit that his muscles, far more defined than I had believed before, impressed me. Rick had told me how strong and aggressive Robbie was during their noontime scrimmages—which made me face up to another problem. Rick actually liked Robbie. I know buddies are entitled to have separate friendships, but it bothered me that a guy I had been running around with since second grade had the nerve to respect someone like Robbie, especially when he knew I hated him.

The strange thing was that wherever I went I looked for Robbie, and when I spotted him, I watched everything he did from a distance. If he looked my way, I pretended not to notice him. I felt like two cents watching Robbie's reactions to Kelly and hers to him, but I couldn't stop myself.

Kelly must have left Robbie behind because she followed me into the gym, sat down next to me and put her hand on my leg. "What's the matter with you?" she asked, looking straight into my eyes.

"Nothing," I said.

"Don't tell me that, Todd Richardson. You know what I mean. The way you treat Robbie." I put my head down. "I can't understand it. I've known you forever and you've never been like this. If you realized a few things, you'd be thankful you're you instead of him."

"I have no idea what you're talking about."

The band began to play. "Todd," she said louder, "you and I have had a lot of fun, haven't we?"

"Sure," I said slowly.

"Remember all those parties in eighth grade?" she continued. "You see, I was talking with my mother about you last fall and she suggested that I ask you over sometime, so I did. It was good seeing you again. We had both grown up so much since that summer at Camp Cherokee."

"You've grown up, you mean. I haven't grown at all."

"Are you worried about your height? I wasn't talking about that kind of growing up."

"You'd worry, too."

"Sometimes I'm afraid I'll grow too tall," Kelly said. "Anyway, I've gotten the idea from Robbie that—"

"Wait a minute! What's he been saying?"

"Robbie's pretty smart about some things." She took my face in her hands and made me look at her. Then she bent to talk into my ear.

Say anything, I thought. Just stay close like this.

"Let's go outside for a few minutes," she said. "Come on." She grabbed my hand and we made our way down between writhing bodies, banners and band members to the floor and then slipped out to the cold, empty lobby. We stood around for a while, saying nothing. Kelly seemed nervous and I felt like a two-year-old, ready to have a tantrum if I heard one more thing I didn't like.

"I've always thought a lot of you," Kelly began, locking her hands behind her.

Right. Now will you come out and tell me you don't like me "that way"?

"We had a good few weeks together. But then Robbie came along. You didn't say anything to me. Robbie said he thought you were upset."

"I don't need his theories. Didn't you know how I felt when I sort of grabbed you that day in my bedroom?" Kelly ignored my question. How could she?

"If I made you think we'd be going together forever, well, I'm sorry. I didn't promise anything, did I? And you didn't promise me. As for that day in your room, I pulled away, remember?"

Why couldn't I ever express myself to her? I began pacing.

"Will you please stop acting this way?"

I looked at her. "I'm really glad you have someone like Robbie to fill you in on everyone's deepest feelings," I said.

"Oh, come off it, Todd. Robbie and I aren't going together, if that's what you want to know. He's hard to pin down. He loves to have fun and he's a great talker. But knowing he's harmless is what makes him so cute."

One fact I was sure of: nothing about Robbie would ever seem cute to me.

Kelly continued. "I remember a few times when you shot your mouth off, like the night you said you could eat an entire giant pizza at the bowling alley, remember?"

"That was years ago. I'm positive I could manage a whole one now."

"One thing Robbie doesn't joke about is that he knows you don't like him."

"Let's drop it, Kelly."

"He wants to be your friend." When she saw my lack of response, she threw up her arms. "All right, I did my best." She walked around, then stopped. "My birthday is today," she said. "I want to invite you to my party, but since Robbie's going to be there, it probably wouldn't be fair to either of you."

"Hardly." How could I have forgotten her birthday? Her parties were always great.

"I just wish you'd change your mind about Robbie." She tried to take my hand. I twisted away.

"Forget it," I said. I started toward the door, then turned. "If you want me at your party, I'll come," I said. "If not, no big deal." I opened the door to the gym, letting in a rush of warm, sweat-sock air.

"Please come," she said, smiling. "I want you to, okay? My house after the game. Things will work out, don't you think?"

I shrugged. "I guess."

That night Rick led the scoring as usual, shooting every time he got the ball, swishing it in no matter where he was. Robbie jumped up and down, waving his towel from the bench, more excited than Coach Smith. Rick was great at drawing fouls, too, and was eight for ten at the free-throw line. I saw Kelly with her girlfriends but forgot even her, yelling "two-two-two" with the rest of the crowd while stabbing fingers at the refs. We won by three points in overtime. Correction:

Rick won by three points. It was the greatest game he ever played.

By the time I got to Kelly's it was almost ten-thirty. I didn't know if others were giving Kelly presents, but I had bought her a record at the all-night market. The lights from her house spilled out onto the snow as I ran up on the front porch. Kelly planted a tiny kiss on my cheek when I handed her the record. "My favorite group!" she cried. "I'm going to play this now."

She took my hand and we went into the rec room, where everyone I had expected to see was there, dancing or stuffing down food. I glanced around. Robbie and Rick hadn't arrived yet. I asked Kelly if she wanted to dance, but when I had her in my arms I felt funny staring at her ear. Two years ago she had raised her hands to put them around my neck. Now she slid them across my shoulders. Actually, I think they drooped down a little. I squeezed her to me. Nothing had changed about her softness, her breasts pushing at me like two foam pillows.

Naturally, Robbie and Rick had to get there at that moment. Everyone gave them the grand welcome, and Kelly left me to join the rest who were slapping Rick's back and shaking his hand.

Then Robbie raised his arms to silence the group. "Listen, all of you," he said. Rick turned off the music and the room of friends fell silent. "I have a present for Kelly. It's not an ordinary present, but one I made especially for her, a custom poem you might say." He had to be joking.

He pulled a wrinkled envelope from his pocket, holding it up so the light hit it as he opened it. He looked shyly at Kelly who seemed excited at the promise of verse. Who was she trying to fool? She loved him like crazy. The current flowing between them was enough to electrocute all bystanders. He proceeded to read her the poem, stumbling over half the words. How could he goof up his own poem? I suppose it was full of roses and moonlight, none of which I really heard. All I recall is that at the end everyone clapped while Kelly rushed over to Robbie, put her arms around him and kissed him the same way that made me shut my eyes as a little kid when I had the misfortune of sitting through a mushy movie scene. I felt knots playing whiffle ball in my stomach.

"Hi, Todd." Diane stood off to the side. I hadn't noticed her before. "What's wrong?" she asked, putting her arms around me. I smelled booze on her.

"Where did you get it?" I made gestures like a drunk. She giggled. "Lloyd Johnson. I came with him."

"You came here with *him*? Do you realize what he is?"

"You're too critical, you know it?"

"Diane, you're high."

"No lectures, no lectures." Diane's black knight sneaked up and tickled her. Silly laughter trilled through the room. I looked away to see Robbie and Kelly glued to each other, barely moving across the floor as they danced. It made me sick.

"You got any more of that stuff?" I asked Lloyd.

"Out in my car. Come on, Richardson."

The only other time I had a drink was one New Year's when I finished a glass of wine my mom had left in the downstairs bathroom. Now, after three swallows of Jack Daniel's, I felt enormously better. Pretty soon I had finished off the whole bottle. I don't know how I drank that much, but suddenly I was horribly sick. I got out of the car, gasping the sharp night air, and stood still and suffered for twenty minutes before going back into the house. In the hall I almost collided with Kelly's dad.

"Everyone having a good time?" he asked.

"Oh yes, sir," I said, trying to focus on his face.

Back at the party I sat in a corner with Rick and Walt who never asked girls to dance. Rick was practically asleep. Kelly and Robbie were still going at it, inch by inch, stopping to kiss or stare at each other every two feet.

"Screw both of them," I muttered.

"What?" Walt asked. He shouldn't have.

"I said, screw them both." So what if my voice was loud? I thought I saw Kelly pause and look at me. "In fact, you can screw everyone in this whole damn place," I yelled, laughing. "Walt, got any beer on you?"

"Gosh no," he said, getting up.

Rick looked at me. "Are you sloshed or something?"

My stomach started to screw up again. Kelly came toward me without Robbie. "I don't want my parents to hear you," she said, her voice cold. "You'd better leave."

"Telling me you don't want him," I said, throwing my arm out. "You can't fool me. How does it feel to lie, Kelly Small? Do you enjoy getting guys hot? There's a name for it. Know what it is?"

Robbie pushed Kelly aside. "Hey, maybe Walt could take you home," he said.

"I'm not going anywhere. You two need a chaperone."

Kelly looked as if she wanted to kill me. Whatever slight affection she held two hours ago had evaporated.

Robbie came closer. "You shouldn't have drunk anything," he whispered. "You're making a bonehead out of yourself. I know what I'm talking about. Drinking doesn't do anyone any good, and when you get up tomorrow you're not going to like yourself very much."

"Go back to your adoring girlfriend and screw her or whatever," I snarled. "That's all you're after anyway."

Kelly burst into tears. "I knew it wouldn't work. How can you say these things? Get out." She wiped her eyes. "My father can't hear any of this."

"Yes, Miss Perfect," I said, attempting to make my way to the hall. I had to get some air. I found the closet, got my jacket and started for the door.

Chapter
10

"Todd . . ."

I looked around to see Robbie standing in the hallway. Everything began to spin.

"Kelly wants to know if she should ask her dad to drive you home."

"Samson, what are you, her personal envoy? For the last time, get your nose out of my business."

"I know you like her a lot. I'm sorry—"

"The hell you are. You've done everything to make sure nothing will ever happen between her and me, and that includes your stupid, cheap-shot poem. Butt out and stay away from me."

Robbie laughed, embarrassed. "I had to write her a poem," he said. "I didn't have any money for a present. I thought I'd have it, but I was wrong. And I didn't realize she'd get so carried away."

"I'll bet you didn't." I opened the door. "You planned it. You work everything to your advantage."

"Wait. I have something to say to you," he said.

"I've got some advice for you, too, but it's unprintable."

"Why don't you give up on Kelly? You remind me of a biting dog that won't quit. You're not her type. She thinks I am, and who am I to argue, so why don't you stop getting worked up when you see us together? You'll get hurt, but if that's what you want . . ."

I slammed the door and ran to him, grabbing his sweater. Isn't this what he wanted, standing there with that smile? "You mean like you hurt Diane, so she's in there with that creep Johnson because you broke your promise?"

"When are you going to believe that I didn't—"

"Never, liar. Don't talk to me about Kelly, ever again." I felt something breaking inside me. "And don't go around telling people about me—what's going on in my head—because you don't know and you never will." I let go.

Robbie took a step backward. His face fell into shadow. "Man, you've got a head on you as big as a watermelon. I'm serious. I can't understand what you think I've done to you. So Kelly likes me. So what? You don't own her. You think I took her away from you? If you want to know the truth, she asked me first. She introduced herself to *me* while you were so-called going together."

"That's a damn lie."

"*She* asked *me* to go skating. I didn't have any money. How was I to ask a lawyer's daughter anywhere?"

"That's not true."

"Let it go, Richardson. After tonight she'll never respect you again."

"I'm so sick of you it stinks," I whispered. Something bitter was working its way up my esophagus. "Get outside. We're going to settle this, or, rather, I'm going to beat your head in."

I reached for him. He stopped me with a firm hand on my wrist. "I'm not fighting a drunk," he said, his voice low. "You don't even know what you're saying. Go home and go to bed."

"So you can go at it with Kelly."

"Shut up, Todd. I'm getting sick of you, too. Look, if you want to settle something, meet me down at the football field at eight tomorrow. At least you'll be making sense."

"I'm not waiting until tomorrow. I . . ."

Kelly, her father and some others appeared in the hallway. "I'm taking you home," Kelly's father said. "You're the last person I figured I'd ever see in this condition."

Kelly stood motionless, her hands held helplessly out from her body. She looked so hurt that I felt immediate crushing shame. Robbie took her hand.

"Tomorrow then," I said to Robbie. He nodded.

"Don't tell my dad anything, okay?" I asked on the way home. "I'm not a drinker, Mr. Small, really. Even one beer does me in."

"That's obvious," he said, "but you did ruin Kelly's party. She's very upset." We had pulled into my driveway. "May I help you in?"

"No, I'll be all right." I opened the car door, almost

falling out. "I'm sorry," I said. "Tell her I'm sorry."

Rick called almost immediately. "You okay?" he asked.

"What do you think? I'm fighting Robbie tomorrow."

"I don't believe it. Where?"

"I'm not saying, but I'll tell you this: he's going down."

Rick laughed. "I hope you have a good dentist. You're going to end up with your teeth knocked out, old buddy."

The next morning my head hurt like hell, but I thought I'd live—until I remembered my agreement with Robbie. Why couldn't I have kept my mouth shut last night? The thought of fighting made me shake. If I didn't show, he'd tell everyone. Maybe we'd talk. But about what? I had nothing more to say to him. The idea of Kelly making the first move to meet Robbie kept bothering me. It just couldn't be true.

He came along Fifth at eight-twenty. To keep warm, I had been jogging around sections of the field where the snow had melted. As he approached I began to feel more uneasy. He looked much stronger than last night in the quiet light of Kelly's house, but his face was still calm. Did that mean he was confident, that I wouldn't stand a chance? Even if I got one dynamic punch in, that would be enough to satisfy me, just one good slug. "One," I said to myself, "one good one."

He walked to within five feet of where I stood and stopped. The air was frosty. Our breaths came out in quick white puffs as we stood on the field, staring at each other.

"I can do better without my jacket," I said, unzipping

it. He didn't answer me, but he took his off and threw it on top of a snowy bench a few feet away. The cold cut into my chest and back like a frozen sword, and I noticed Robbie beginning to shiver, although he was trying to conceal it.

A hint of a smile played on his lips as he slipped his hands into his pants pockets. He actually believed he was going to cream me. Of all the egotistical jerks I had come across! I couldn't wait to punch the crummy smile off his face.

In one swift motion I lunged at him, knocking him onto his back. He seemed strangely light. This is going to be easy, I thought. His black hair, speckled with snow, stuck out at several angles. He's a pansy, I thought. What if I kill him? But I wanted to, or at least mess him up a lot, especially that good-looking face of his. What was I waiting for?

"This is for Kelly," I said. Raising myself, I hit him in the mouth, opening the left side of his upper lip. He turned his head sideways, the blood from his mouth dripping onto the snow. He didn't try to get up. He wasn't fighting back. Something inside my head issued a warning.

"I'll give you a chance," I said gruffly, getting off him. "Get up." I just couldn't make hamburger of him.

Looking at me the whole time, he stood slowly, rubbing his raw hands against his sweater. He didn't speak. He stood there stiffly, his lip beginning to swell. I felt strange. My fury changed to bewilderment.

No, I came here to take care of things.

Again I attacked him, sending him back down. My stomach grabbed. "This one's for Diane," I said, hitting him on the chin and side of his face. Another blow I tried missed. But he just lay there looking at me without making a sound. "You're not fighting," I said. "We came here to fight. Get up."

He stood again and stumbled forward. I was breathing so hard that my heart was hammering and I could hear the blood gushing through my ears. I hit him again in the face. It was crazy. Blood covered it now, but this time Robbie didn't fall down. He stood with his hands at his sides, staring at me. I punched him again and again until at last he fell backward. I heard him groan.

"Why won't you fight?" I yelled, my spit flying all over the place.

He struggled to sit up, wiping blood on the sleeve of his sweater. The sweater was light blue and his blood turned purple against it.

"What's the matter with you?"

"I don't want to fight," he said, his voice barely audible.

"That's what the hell we came out here for, isn't it?"

"I don't want to fight you," he repeated. "I never said I would."

"You chicken, you—fag. I should have known." I thrust my foot into a snowdrift, sending a white spray into the wind. "So you're probably going to tell everyone about this and make people feel sorry for you, mostly Kelly. It figures. I don't have any idea what your game is, but let me know when you're ready to cut out this crap. You may have Kelly on your side, but you're not taking my position on the team. And my grandpa. Stay away from him. Don't go near him again."

He stared at me, silent. It hurt to breathe. I wanted him to at least take a cut at me, but I knew he wouldn't. I averted my eyes, then looked back at him. He bowed his head and got up and went to pick up his jacket, stumbling over a rock.

"A game," he said with his back to me. The wind had picked up. The piercing cold stung my eyes. He turned to face me again. "All right," he said, his eyes huge and black against the blood on his face. "It was a game, a big put-on."

He began to cough, and I wondered when he was going to stop. "I was lonely and bored when I moved here. Every time we move, it's the same thing—no friends. People told me you were a great guy. I wanted to be like you, so I tried in my own way—I guess it wasn't any good—to get to know you." He sank down on the bench. "I didn't mean to cause you any trouble. I came to tell you that. I only wanted to be your friend."

"You . . ." came out in a croak. My feet felt like frozen bricks. Nothing was making any sense. After retrieving my jacket, I pulled it on and zipped it up. When I finished, Robbie stretched his right arm toward me. What was he doing, trying to shake hands?

I couldn't stop myself, even though I wanted to. It was like standing outside my body watching myself talk. "My friend?" I laughed. "You've got to be crazy. You're the last person I'd ever want to be friends with."

Avoiding his eyes, I walked off the field, leaving him sitting on the bench, while my heart pushed pain through my chest. I didn't look back, but as I walked past the school and down the road toward home, something colder than the air stabbed me. I gazed at the dead gray sky. Then I vomited into the snow. What could I do or say now? How had this whole thing become such a mess? Robbie had never meant me any harm. I knew that now, but once you've made a terrible mistake, you can never go back.

I had been wrong about Robbie. I was wrong and everyone else was right.

Chapter
11

Monday morning I saw him in algebra. His lip was still swollen. Even from a distance it looked like he'd have some kind of scar where I had knocked it open. I turned once and saw his eyes staring ahead. For a second his glance rested on me, then switched to the other side of the room.

All Sunday I had thought about it. I worried more about what I had done to Robbie than about my status with Kelly. That was hopeless. She would hate me forever.

Apologizing wouldn't help. I had gone too far. My grandpa's words kept coming back to me. But why did Robbie need Grandpa and me? Why did he keep trying when I had rejected him over and over? As much as he had been hanging around, I knew very little about him. Would knowing more have made a difference?

I couldn't talk to Mom or Grandpa about it, either. My

mother freaked out when I watched boxing on TV, and my grandpa just wouldn't understand.

At noon, before the lunch line opened, I slouched alone with my untouched tray. Robbie sat a couple of tables away with Diane. After a while she got up and came over. "I didn't realize you were so strong," she said, sighing. "You whaled on Robbie something awful."

"I don't want to talk about it," I said. "I want to forget it."

"We were all sure you'd get murdered. That's what all the guys at the party said. What I wanted to tell you is I'm sorry Lloyd let you have that whiskey. If I wasn't drunk, I wouldn't have let him."

"I didn't have to take it. It wasn't Lloyd's fault."

"I still feel bad that Robbie got banged up. Nothing against you. You had reasons, I guess, but his poor face, Todd."

"I thought you'd be glad, since he dropped you and took Kelly to that dance when you asked him first." Diane blushed and turned her head. "You mean you weren't mad at him?" I didn't understand her. She had to be either a martyr or an idiot. If Robbie had done one bad deed, dumping Diane was it.

"You said you knew what happened."

"Sure. You asked Robbie to the dance. He agreed. Kelly asked him later and he told you he was taking her instead."

"That's not what happened."

"What are you talking about?"

Diane fidgeted with her fingernails, then started biting one. "I only said I asked him," she whispered. "Actually, I was too scared to. I was trying to get up the nerve, but then I heard Kelly had asked him."

"Great," I said under my breath.

"Todd, Robbie's so quiet. I've never seen him this way. Everyone at East knows you guys fought, but no one found out what happened. He won't say a word."

I watched him get up and empty his tray. He disappeared into the dish room.

"Are you mad at me?" Diane asked. "Did I cause trouble? Did I?"

My face must have shown my emotions because she started to cry.

"Diane, whatever happened between Robbie and me was my fault, not yours," I said.

"Don't hate him," she said, wiping her nose.

"I regret everything I said and did, but there's no way I can fix things now." I got up and took my untouched food away. Diane followed closely behind.

"You mean you're not mad?" she asked. "Everyone's sure you hate his guts."

I got into position and grabbed the serving spoon, waiting for the first person through the line to complain about the succotash.

"You forgot your apron," Diane said. I began to dish out vegetables. "Are you going to make up with him?"

"Oh crap, Diane," I said, "just leave me alone. Guys don't make up. That sounds imbecilic."

During the next two days I avoided everyone. Friends tried to talk to me about the fight, but I put them off.

Robbie, evidently, was still silent. No one knew anything. At home I dodged Mom and Grandpa and stayed in my room at night. Nothing mattered. I listened to music and let my schoolwork go. One night I went into the den to try to talk to Dad, but there was nothing to say. I don't know which one of us was more depressed.

Thursday night Grandpa came to my room. "Knock-knock," he said.

As soon as I saw his wide face and scraggly white hair I felt some kind of relief. "I know what you're going to say," I warned him.

"Was I going to say something?" He pretended innocence. "I haven't seen you lately. Have you gone into hiding, or did I offend you by calling you a spoiled brat? You are, you know."

"I know."

He came in and sat on my bed. "You don't have to tell me anything." I shrugged. "But I have a suspicion something happened to knock your props loose."

"Maybe."

"I assume it might concern Robbie."

"I thought you said I didn't have to tell you anything."

"I think it has to do with Robbie because he hasn't been around lately. Any ideas why?"

A noise stirred in my throat. Grandpa's eyes brightened. I sat on my lumpy rug, picking at a loose strand. He waited. We sat, me picking, Grandpa looking out the window. I pulled at the thread until it came loose. Then I started chewing on it.

"Grandpa," I said finally, "I made a mistake—not just

a simple mistake—a *rotten* mistake." He nodded. "I don't want to get into it, but I need to square things with Robbie. The thing is I can't. I don't know how."

"You're afraid. Yep, that's a sticky one."

"I've been unfair," I said.

"Yes."

"What do you think I should do?"

"Well, since I have no idea what happened, I don't think I can give any advice."

I got up and started to walk around. "Robbie and I got into a fight."

"I figured that."

"I beat him up."

"Now, that's a surprise."

"He let me do it. He stood there and allowed me to punch his lights out. It reminds me of the only time I ever beat David James in the mile. You know, the kid who set the state record last year?"

"You beat *him?*"

"He fell down."

Grandpa cleared his voice. "I see your point."

"He didn't fight back. He stood there like a zombie and when it was over he said—well, he tried to shake hands or something. I mean, I split his lip and gave him a black eye. I had a reason—I thought I did—because of Kelly. At her party she and he were practically doing it standing up, and I got drunk and angry and called them names, and that's when I told Robbie I was going to fight him. He said we could talk, but when we met the next day I didn't give him a chance. I started in on him."

"Is it just because of the girl?"

"It's her and a lot of other things."

"How do you feel about Robbie now?"

"I don't hate him anymore," I said. "I don't like him, either."

"You don't even know him," Grandpa said.

"I'm not sure I want to. Grandpa, what do I do now?"

Grandpa didn't give advice. He simply said, "You can figure it out, Todd."

I was back at the beginning.

Chapter
12

When I got home on the day Dad went to the hospital, I opened the door to an unsettling quiet. I called patient information, but the receptionist couldn't tell me anything. I felt left out. I thought for sure Grandpa would call, but the phone sat like a rock on the table in the den.

At five Grandpa came home. "He's fine," he said. "We'll go over tonight for a bit." I didn't say anything. "Well, do we eat out or shall we struggle in the kitchen?" Grandpa knew I was pissed. "I can cook scrambled eggs."

"I'm not eating."

"I sure as hell am." He went into the kitchen. I heard chopping and rattling and the oven door slamming. One thing I knew. You don't make scrambled eggs in the oven.

I went to investigate. Grandpa had stuff strewn all

over the counter. He had dropped an egg on the floor and was smearing it on the tile in an effort to wipe it up. I got out some plates.

"On the farm last summer I don't remember you being this—"

"Messy? Guess I'm a little nervous like you."

"I'm not nervous. You said Dad's okay, didn't you?"

The doorbell rang. "Get that," Grandpa said. "Or do you want to cook?"

When I pulled open the door, Robbie stood in the entryway, his hands in his pockets. "I came to pay you," he said. "We had a deal."

"Come on in," I said.

He stepped inside and glanced around. "Is your grandpa here? I don't want him to see me." Robbie looked terrible, the cut at the side of his mouth making him tough. "How much?" he asked, his eyes darker than ever.

"I'm . . . not going to charge you," I said, barely getting the words out. "And Grandpa knows. He's the only one who does."

He nodded. "I heard your dad had his operation. He okay?" When I said yes, he brought a hand out of one pocket and held out a twenty-dollar bill. "Here," he said. "I owe it to you. If you want more, tell me."

"I'm not taking anything."

He dropped the money then, and I watched it zigzag to the floor. "See you 'round," he said, starting for the door.

"Wait."

Slowly he turned his head. "What do you want?" he asked. His face was stone.

"I found out that you—that you told the truth about Diane. I want you to know. She, well, admitted she lied to me. I didn't think she'd do that."

He paused for a moment, then walked out the door without a word. The money lay on the floor by my feet. I picked it up and ran to my room. On the table by the side of my bed was a Bible. I slipped the money between its thin pages. That night I decided I'd spend it only if I was able to make things right with Robbie.

Why can't we ever go back, rerun our lives and take out the bad parts? I wondered, shaking my head. Why couldn't Robbie have been coming over for his lesson, joking and jumping around like he had before? No scar or silence between us like there was now. Why did I have to screw up everything in the first place? We might have become friends if I had kept cool about Kelly. A guy with a personality like that didn't come along very often, especially one who seemed to have so much fun. Some good times could have rubbed off on me, too, if I hadn't been so stupid. I mean, when I thought back, Robbie hadn't done one thing to me. All the time, I was seeing in him what my mind told me to see. I wondered what he was really like, but now that I wanted to know I'd probably never find out. I walked slowly down the stairs to the kitchen, anything but hungry.

At the hospital I was allowed in Dad's room for five minutes. He had tubes stuck in and out everywhere.

"How can anyone look that bad?" I asked Grandpa. "It's almost like he's . . ."

"The hardest part will be keeping him from jumping right back to work again. He didn't take after me that way. I've always been such an easygoing S.O.B."

"An energetic, easygoing S.O.B."

"Must be something chemical. You're like him, Todd—a perfectionist. People had better live up to your expectations or else. You don't slow down any more than he does."

"Are you serious? Am I going to end up like this?"

"Now, if I were God, I'd tell you. Come on. Let's go out in the hall." Outside the door he put his arm around me. "Promise me you won't go into insurance. What a bore. Now farming, there's the good life."

"I know you miss it."

"I have a pile of money coming if I sell the place. I could do some traveling when this whole thing is over. Can you believe I've only been in two states in my life?" Grandpa got that shiny glow in his eyes. "Let's walk," he said. "I've been thinking. When you graduate, let's you and I go to Europe. What do you say to that?"

"I've always sort of wanted to go to Alaska," I said.

"Okay, Alaska sounds good to me."

"*Then* Europe."

Grandpa laughed. "I was wondering," he said, "how things are between you and Robbie."

"Oh," I said, sighing. "That was him at the door tonight. I think he hates me now more than I ever hated him."

95

"I heard you talking. I'm a terrible old snoop. But you made an attempt. It was a start. He's probably more upset with himself for not beating you up."

In the days following Dad's return home Grandpa, Mom and I did everything to make Dad comfortable, but strangely, he began to act as if his life was over. When I went into his room to see him, he'd turn his head and stare out the window.

I tried to cheer him up any way I could. One day I talked about our most eventful trip to the north woods. "I was thinking of that time we went out with Pete to bag a deer," I said, "and ended up with a bear. Wow! Wasn't that some fantastic day? I mean, I've used it at least three times for first-person essays."

I took a big bite out of my thumbnail. Dad sat on his bed, rubbing his hands together, not even looking my way.

"Who would have thought that big old thing'd show up and come at us like that? Pete telling me to get behind a tree, except we didn't happen to be anywhere near one at the time. If I hadn't been so scared, the whole experience would have been funny—the bear running like crazy, coming straight for me . . ."

Nothing. I took a deep breath and let it out slowly. Dad shifted. I leaned forward.

"You sure were my big hero that day. I bragged for weeks about how brave you were, how you saved me." The thing I didn't mention to my friends, however, was how Dad had come into my room every night after that for weeks to calm me down. I had terrible nightmares about getting mauled to death and eaten by the bear.

"Those dreams will go away one day," my dad assured me. They did.

"Do you remember?" I asked, scratching my head. "That's stupid. No one could ever forget a day like that. Well, what shall we talk about now?"

Dad turned his face, and just for a moment his eyes met mine. "I'm tired," was all he said.

When Dr. Golden and Mom talked over the phone, I heard her whisper something about post-operative depression. I saw her cry. I always thought Grandpa could make it through any crisis, but my father stumped even him. I'd hear him teasing, begging and ordering Dad to get up and go downstairs, but it didn't do any good. The situation was turning into a real nightmare, and this time no one could tell me it would go away.

I guess it was around that time that I began to miss assignments and started sleeping or daydreaming in class. I even argued with teachers. At school I hardly talked to anyone. Rick and I hadn't stopped by the DQ in almost three months. Since I still saw Diane every day, she asked a million times what was wrong. I told her to leave me alone.

One day I slid a note through one of the vents in Kelly's locker.

Dear Kelly,
That wasn't me at your party.
It was a jealous, drunk jerk who hopes to turn back into a person someday.

Will you forgive me? I know it's him for good, but do you think you could possibly stop hating me?

Love,
Todd

I tried to get my finger in there and take it back, but my finger was too big.

Kelly went right on as if I'd never written a thing, which made me even more depressed. Looking back, I wondered if she had approached Robbie first, but it didn't matter anymore. I still felt the same way about her, and she would never feel anything for me again. Even so, I watched her and Robbie, usually from a hiding place. After a while they were all I thought about. I could almost guess what he was saying to her when he touched her arm in a certain way, and when she threw her head back and laughed, I knew he must be telling her one of his fish stories. When I got up every morning, I planned my strategy so that I'd be at their places without their knowing.

One afternoon I was summoned to the office. "I'd like to talk with you, Todd. Do you mind?" Mrs. Callum, the school psychologist, met me inside the office door.

"No," I said, totally surprised. I'd never seen her office. The room was stuffed with plants and books. All kinds of pictures hung on the wall. There was no desk, just two chairs. She motioned me to one of them, then sat herself.

"Have I done something wrong?" I asked.

Mrs. Callum smiled one of those professional smiles,

the kind that make you suspicious, even though she looked terrific. A lot of guys talked about inventing problems to get into her office.

"Are you comfortable?" she asked.

"Sure." *Like a cat stuck up a chimney*.

"Todd, I'm going to ask you directly. Are you taking drugs?"

"No," I said. I glanced over at her file cabinet covered with decals.

"One of your teachers thought enough of you to tell me that your work is suffering. That and the fact you have been withdrawn alarmed your teacher. Your other instructors confirmed the report. When a person changes radically, the determinant is often drug use. But you say you don't do drugs."

"No."

"Do you want to talk about anything? I'm here to help."

"No," I said louder.

Mrs. Callum looked annoyed. I didn't want her to dislike me. "We don't have to talk today. I'd like you to think about seeing me again, though."

"I don't know why," I said. "It's nothing you could do anything about."

"What makes you so sure?"

I shrugged. "It's my dad." I saw her thoughts: a problem at home, like so many others. It was none of her business. She probably thought he was an alcoholic or something.

I sat there going over every plant, every picture. I

wanted to leave. Who had ratted? Mr. Nash. I never opened my mouth in his class anymore, and my test grades stunk.

I got up. "I can work through my own problems," I said. "Thanks anyway."

"I know you think you should, but sometimes solutions become more apparent as you talk them over. I'm not here to pry, and I never ask a student to meet with me unless—"

"He's messed up," I said.

"Will you come back Thursday?"

"I don't know."

"We'll leave it open then. I'll be here at this time."

"You aren't going to call my mom, are you? She couldn't take it."

"Of course not," she said. "Not at this point."

I left, feeling like some kind of emotional cripple. As I walked down the hall I wanted to cry. Then for some reason I stopped and glanced back over my shoulder. I saw Robbie Samson entering Mrs. Callum's office.

Chapter
13

I wish I could say things improved, but I can't. My spirits stayed as dreary as the last rainy days of March. My father continued to behave like a hermit, my mom become more nervous and my grandpa stomped around the house like an angry elephant.

For some reason I went back to Mrs. Callum. Since nobody at home wanted to talk about Dad, I wondered if she might understand what was going on with him.

"Robbie Samson comes here, too, doesn't he?" I asked.

"Would you want him to know *you're* here?" she said. "There's nothing shameful about it, but many don't like to imagine they're weak. It's strength to talk, the best way to deal with problems. When you keep them bottled up— bam! You may be in for a whole mountain of problems."

"I don't feel sick or anything," I said. "Mostly I'm confused. This year has been crummy. Not that I expect everything to go my way. It's just that nothing has."

For all my determination not to, I found myself yakking like a magpie. Sure, Mrs. Callum had this great body, and she turned out to be about the nicest person I ever met, but it was something else. I had to talk and she was the only one I could unload on.

"I go to his room," I said. "He's in the guest room now. I go over to his bed where he sits, his face turned away, and I say, 'Dad, how are you doing?' because I can't think of anything else, and he doesn't even answer me. So later I bring him his dinner and he stares at it, that's all. What's the matter with him? My mom goes around like she's been slapped in the face, and my grandpa—"

I ranted for nearly an entire period.

"Why don't you come back, say, next Thursday?" Mrs. Callum said.

"I'm pretty bad off, huh?"

She laughed. "Actually, I enjoy talking to you, Todd."

"But I do all the talking."

"You're quite a young man, do you know that?"

I went down the hall afterward thinking, "quite a young man." Quite what? Quite wonderful? Quite crazy? Stupid? Handsome? Boring?

Baseball tryouts began the next Monday. I came home, put on a pair of baseball pants, got out my cleats and walked past Mom, who was waiting for Dr. Golden. As I got my glove and went out, I wondered why he was making a house call. Still, I had to get away fast. There was no way being sick was going to stop baseball for me.

"Todd?" Kelly stood on the lawn. My heart rate quadrupled. "I want to talk to you," she said. "I heard about your dad. I'm really sorry!" The words came gushing out and her face turned scarlet. "Oh, Todd," she said, "that's not what I came here for. I want—let's not be mad at each other anymore."

"I was never mad at you."

"I know. There are a thousand things I want to say. I shouldn't have made such a big deal out of that night. You wouldn't have said any of those things if you hadn't been drinking."

"That's for sure."

"Actually, it's you that should forgive me. What I did wasn't right. Before the party. I'm ashamed, really ashamed of myself."

"You don't have to explain anything. It's over. You went with me to get Robbie, right? It's okay. If you would have told me what you wanted, I'd have understood, though."

"I didn't go with you to get him. I met Robbie a week after the dance you and I went to. I never meant to hurt you. I always thought we were more or less just friends, because you never told me how much you cared, and I found out the hard way the night of the party."

"I deserved a nomination for jackass of the year."

"Robbie wasn't going to take me skating when I asked him because he didn't want to interfere, so I told him you wouldn't care. It was a mistake. I should have told the truth." Kelly turned away from me. "And at the party, the way I acted with Robbie, like you didn't have any feelings at all. It was so unfair. Why do you always have to hurt someone first before you learn a lesson?"

"What I did was worse," I said. "I'd give anything to change that night." Merely being near the person you love makes you want to do all kinds of illogical things. Regardless, I kept my hands at my sides.

"In a way I wish it was you," she said. "You're the kind of person everyone likes." She looked at me sideways. "I do love you, Todd, but in another way."

My stomach rolled. "Don't be silly," I said.

"It's true. I know you, but I don't know Robbie at all. He scares me sometimes with his sad looks when he doesn't think I'm watching."

"I'm not sure what you mean," I said. But I did know in a way. Something had to be happening to him with those trips to Mrs. Callum's office. What was the matter with him?

"I can tell you don't hate Robbie anymore," Kelly said. "Let's walk, okay?"

She took my hand and we started down the sidewalk. It was full of those caterpillar-like things from the budding trees.

"Kelly?" I said after a block of silence. "Why do you— I mean, what makes people love a certain person anyway? Oh, forget it." I felt my face go red.

"You mean why do I love Robbie? You'll think I'm crazy, but if you get to know him, you'll find out. There's something about him."

"Come on, Kelly," I said, making a face.

"You're cute when you look like that." She reached over and kissed my cheek. I wanted to put my arms around her. "I only meant that you understand people. Shall I tell you some things about him?" I shrugged. "He puts on a big act." I was surprised she saw it, too. "He's had it bad. He doesn't complain, but I know he's hurt, only he doesn't want anyone to know it."

"But he told you."

"Not really. I kind of pressured him until he trusted me, but there's more to it. From what he said he's not wanted by anybody—his family, I mean. His mother had him with her after her divorce, and when he was ten she decided to get remarried, but her fiancé didn't want Robbie. So she tried to find his father. It was pretty hard, since she hadn't kept in touch with him. But she had to find Mr. Samson because her boyfriend said it was either him or Robbie. Isn't that just terrible?"

"And then?"

"She located him back east. He wasn't too thrilled, but he took Robbie."

"That kind of thing must happen to a lot of kids. I don't see why it should be a big problem."

"Maybe," Kelly said, frowning, "but for Robbie it is."

We had reached my house again. Kelly sank down on the grass next to the sidewalk. She lay back, raising her arms over her head. She looked up at me through lacy eyelashes as I sat beside her, her blond streaky hair lying tangled over the grass. "Whatever happened the day you fought Robbie?" she asked.

"If he didn't tell you about it, I'd rather not either." I watched a little kid chase a cat down the block. "It was a bad day in my life." She looked away, pouting. "Anyway, I have to go to baseball practice right now," I said.

She sighed and sat up. "All right. Walk with me part-way?"

Chapter

14

As I got to the field, I realized I hadn't mentally prepared myself for this day. The first person I saw was Rick, swinging a bat. Some of the other guys played catch. Robbie stood to the side, dressed in a miserable, beat-up pair of baseball pants and a purple baseball hat. He nodded slightly when he saw me. Even though we both still worked in the cafeteria, we never spoke unless we had to discuss dishes and spoons, and then it was little more than a few mumbles.

Coach Hal Resen had us put our names down on his clipboard list with our intended position. When the clipboard came to me, I saw that Robbie had printed his name and second base as his choice. I wrote "Todd R., short." What made me do it I've wondered to this day.

"Okay," Resen said in his gravelly voice, "will the following boys take the positions they've chosen? We'll do some fielding, then some hitting. Today's a warm-up.

Rick, Walt, Todd, Phil, Ken, Robbie . . ." He continued the list as we ran out on the field. Ken had the ball and started tossing it around. Robbie caught it and turned to throw it to me.

"What are you doing at short?" he yelled, hurling it hard at me.

I threw it back harder. "I figured I was too good for second," I shot back. "Decided to move up."

"If you keep throwing like a girl, you'll get put back in Little League."

"Hey, how about over here?" Rick stood at third. Robbie threw the ball to him with an expert snap of the wrist. Rick flung it to first.

"I'm going to hit to you," Resen called. "We'll start with first."

When he got to second, Robbie picked up the grounders casually, as if selecting eggs. Then he bulleted them to the catcher or first baseman, whichever Resen called.

I missed the first two balls.

"Come on, Richardson," Resen screamed. "You're not a croquet hoop."

Fortunately, I caught most of the rest, but my face stayed hot for the remainder of practice. I didn't do a bad job hitting, despite my nervousness and the fact that Robbie was whacking baseballs all over the field.

Afterward, Resen had us run a mile, and that's when I nearly passed out. By the time I got home my whole body shook and I stood wasted under the shower.

"Grandpa, can you hit?" I asked at dinner.

"Flies or mosquitoes? Oh, do you mean a baseball?"

It was no joke.

"Richardson, are you wearing a blindfold?" The coach asked me the next afternoon. I had just fumbled another grounder. Minutes before I had overthrown first. Robbie shot some remark at me that I didn't catch. I began to think my mono had come back to haunt me.

As soon as we began running the mile Robbie started in on me. "You wouldn't have made our team in Chicago," he said. "Back there, if you couldn't catch the ball, you went out for Ping-Pong."

I was panting so hard I could barely talk. "Samson, when I get back to normal," I said, "I'll be better than you ever were."

"Sure, if Resen gives you a two-foot custom mitt."

"You haven't seen me in top form. In a few weeks you'll be jealous, but I'll go easy on you so you won't be too knocked out of shape."

For the first time since the fight, Robbie smiled. He tilted back his head and laughed his deep laugh, almost losing his hat. "You talk baseball like you serve food in the cafeteria," he said. "You really pile on the crap." He took off ahead of me.

"Yeah?" I called between gasps. "Your brain is tantamount to a block of cement with a leak in it."

He turned his head. "I'd rather be an athletic genius than a guy who has to show off with words just because he can't do anything else. When I'm earning six figures, it won't matter what I say."

I caught up with him again. "Ha! You'll be one of those dudes on TV who says, 'Well-uh, but-uh, ya know' every other word."

"So you admit I'm good. Makes me proud."

"You're good all right. I may pile on the crap, but you dish out a ton of baloney. Maybe you can try for one of those shaving cream commercials. Of course, you'll have to grow something on your face first. Think you might someday?"

"I wouldn't talk. Anyway, I'll be rich and you'll wish you'd gotten my autograph."

One thing I knew: I was going to have to work my butt off to make the team at all. My body felt like leather pulled over creaky bedsprings. Every muscle hurt and I was so tired I walked in without saying hello, went to my room and collapsed on the bed. Grandpa came in later and woke me up.

"Todd," he said, sitting on the bed next to me, "you don't look good."

"I've got to make the team . . . work hard . . ."

"You might have to settle for the junior varsity."

"Never!"

"It's important, but—"

"You'd be proud of Robbie," I said. "He's everything he said he was."

"Good." Grandpa looked down at his hands. "Did you know Dr. Golden was here to see your dad yesterday? I didn't want to bring this up last night, but he thinks Henry needs some psychiatric treatment."

"I think so, too," I said. The old panic returned. "We tried everything."

"We did," he said, "but it's not enough. Anne finally agreed today to have him taken to Fall Hill."

"But that's the nut hatch!" I cried, jumping up. "He isn't that sick."

"Dr. Golden told us that he will be put in the residential section for people with nervous breakdowns or severe depressions."

"But why does he have to go there? I don't understand."

"There's a question of—some suicidal talk."

"I don't believe it."

"He can get antidepressant drugs there. I think it's a good thing."

"Grandpa," I said in a wavering voice, "I've been seeing the school psychologist."

He stood straight up from the bed. "What for? There's nothing wrong with you."

I grabbed his arm. "She called because of my grades. It's been okay."

Grandpa lowered himself to the bed again. "Maybe the whole bunch of us is crazy. Think she'll talk to me? She a dish or one of those horn-rimmed jobs?"

I laughed. "She's pretty, all right."

The ambulance pulled up to our house at seven-thirty. I heard it backing into the driveway. The attendants weren't wearing white jackets or anything, and they didn't carry a stretcher. Mom was a shaky mess. Nobody said anything. I felt empty. Grandpa and the men went upstairs, and a few minutes later my dad came down with them, fully dressed. Dad didn't look at anyone, even when Mom said, "Hank, dear," and touched his arm.

"See you soon, Dad," I said.

He stared at me. Then he said, "Don't bother to come. I don't want to see anyone."

Then they left. I couldn't believe any of it.

Sometimes you think of bizarre things at times like this. As I walked to school the next day, I remembered the Saturday morning Dad took me to the sporting goods store and bought me my first glove.

"How do you like this one? That one?" he asked, letting me take as long as I wanted to decide. He seemed excited that I was finally big enough for baseball, and when we got home we went right out in the backyard where he played catch with me and taught me the best way to hit the ball. I don't know which of us had the most fun.

"This here is going to be one hell of a ballplayer someday," Grandpa told Dad when I got better and was playing Little League. He thumped my back with one big hand and pumped Dad's hand with the other.

"You bet," my dad said. "Better than I ever was."

I thought of freshman ball. I had been at my peak last year, and Dad hadn't attended one game.

Practice went worse that day. My thoughts lingered on Dad's blank expression and the way the ambulance had disappeared around the corner at the end of the street.

Resen cornered me after practice. "Richardson, what's happening to your technique?" he asked. "You don't look like you used to out there."

"Sorry," I said.

"You act disinterested. If you want to play on this team, I have to see effort and improvement."

How could I try any harder?

I started home alone. It was a while before I noticed Robbie walking beside me. "You're lousy," he said. "You're as bad at baseball as I am at math."

"I'm not that bad," I said. "I have a lot on my mind, that's all."

"You think you have problems. You have a great family, a fancy house, everything you could possibly want, and—"

"My dad had to go to Fall Hill this morning," I said.

"What's Fall Hill?"

"A mental institution."

"Huh?" He stopped walking.

"He wouldn't do anything after his operation. He was supposed to get into those exercises. And he wouldn't talk to anyone—stuff like that. Now he has to get well."

Robbie pulled off his purple hat. We started to walk again. He took a deep breath and blew it out. "Well, I can't help you with your dad," he said, "because my father and I have about the worst relationship in the world. But there's something I can do."

"What would you want to do for me?"

"Make a baseball player out of you."

"I told you, I—"

"Yeah, I know what you said, but the truth is you're not going to make the varsity unless you improve, problems or not."

"You want me on the team? Why?"

He didn't answer my question. Instead he said, "We're going to practice every night that I don't have to work. Understand, Professor?"

I couldn't believe him. "All right," I mumbled, "but I don't see—"

"Beginning with tonight. Look, you don't have any time to waste. Cuts are next Friday." We had reached my street. "I'll meet you back down there at six-thirty," he said. "Rick'll be there, too. He could use some improvement himself."

"Now, wait a minute."

"You'd better try, or—"

"Or what, Samson?" I couldn't help it. I smiled at him.

"Or I'll beat your brains in, and since that's all you've got going for you, you'd be a total waste without them."

I watched as he walked off in his threadbare, grass-stained baseball pants and ugly purple hat.

Chapter
15

That night Mom told me we wouldn't be able to see Dad for two weeks and only then if he was beginning to respond. Dr. Golden felt optimistic about Dad, that it shouldn't take more than a month or two to "correct things."

I told Mrs. Callum. "You seem relieved," she said.

"At least I know that something's being done for him now. And there's baseball. I'm trying to make the varsity. Takes my mind off things."

The night before, Rick and Robbie wouldn't let me go home until it was dark and we couldn't see the ball anymore. I fell asleep in my practice clothes and woke up in the morning with dirt caked on my mouth.

"This may seem unrelated, but do you have a girlfriend, Todd?" Mrs. Callum asked.

"I'm not gay, if that's what you mean."

"That's not why I asked."

"I thought I had one once. You know, the old unrequited love story. I'm one of those one-woman men, I guess, because it's been her for three years."

We talked some more, and then Mrs. Callum asked me to come back in three weeks. "But stop in or call me at home if you need to, okay?"

"You mean I'm all well now?" I asked.

"Don't be so dramatic. You know what the problem was, and now that your grades are moving up, you're heading back to the barn. Rough times? Sure, and that's when I want you to call. Promise?"

"Are Robbie's problems heavy? I mean, he's helping me with baseball and everything. Is he still seeing you?"

She took my hand. "I can't discuss him," she said.

"Well, whatever's bothering him, I hope you're helping."

"I'm glad I got a chance to talk to you," she said, smiling.

Not only did I show up for regular practice the next four days, but Rick and Robbie had me on the field every morning and every night. Robbie must have knocked a hundred whizzing grounders at me per session, yelling insults when I missed one. Rick stood fast at first to catch my throws, later pitching to me if Rob had to work.

None of the other guys trying out knew about these secret sessions. Resen gave me an encouraging nod on Wednesday, and Thursday night after our evening practice Robbie came up to me. "You're going to make it," he said.

"Look . . ." I dug at the dirt with one of my cleats. "I just wanted to thank you—you know—for all your help. I admit I sure needed it."

"I wanted you to get short over Rodney McAfree and you will. I hate his guts." He started off.

It took a minute for his statement to register. "For crying out loud," I said, "is that why you did it, because of McAfree?"

He turned, giving me a half smile.

"You jerk," I said.

"What did you expect?" His voice was flat. "I don't play my best with people I hate."

"Oh yeah? What about me?"

Robbie laughed, threw his glove in the air and caught it behind his back. "Guess you must be one inch ahead of McAfree," he said as he continued off toward his part of town.

The next afternoon Rick and I went to the bulletin board outside Resen's office. I was in; McAfree was out. Seeing my name on the roster stirred nothing wonderful in me. It was like having studied hard for a test and passing with a D.

"I wonder if he'll put me on first or third," Rick said. "Ken's going to end up in the outfield, what do you want to bet?"

"I'm going to ask Coach to put me there," I said.

Rick's face changed. "Why? After all we—oh no. Don't tell me. You and Robbie are going at it again."

"He wanted me to make short over Rod because he hates him. He used me."

Rick shrugged. "So? You made the varsity, didn't you? I was sort of hoping when we got on the team together we'd all be friends."

"And Cinderella and the prince lived happily ever after. Robbie and I are not destined to get along, Rick. It's like a natural law—gravity, birth, death. You can't change some things."

Mom went to Fall Hill on Saturday to see Dad. Grandpa and I cooked an elaborate dinner of veal scallopini from *The Glorious Foods of Italy*. We even made spumoni for dessert.

Mom returned at six, drained and upset.

"He isn't doing well," Grandpa stated. "If only I'd kept him on the farm."

Mom took off her jacket. "He's not talking," she said. "He stares at the wall. Now he's allergic to the antidepressant drug." Her voice broke. "I'm sorry. I'm going up to my room."

"No, Mom," I said, remembering Mrs. Callum's warning about talking things out. "Come on, let it go. I care about Dad a lot and I'm scared, too."

Nobody said anything. Mom blinked at me. "I wanted to protect you," she said.

"You act like I'm dumb or something." I looked down. "When can I see him?"

Mom shook her head. "I don't think you should for a while."

"I want to go next weekend," I said.

"Let him," said Grandpa.

"His illness started a long time ago, didn't it?" I asked. "I've been thinking. He acted funny before the operation."

"I knew something was wrong a year ago," my mother

said, "but I thought he was worried about his heart condition. Now I know differently."

"Is it—I mean, could it be me?"

"Oh, honey, of course not." She walked over and hugged me. I started to pull away, but then I thought maybe she needed a hug more than I did. "Whatever it is, someone will find the answer."

"Grandpa and I made something good for dinner. Think you can eat? I know I'm ready."

Mom patted her little round stomach. "Does this look like it needs food?"

"Come on, Annie," Grandpa said, swinging a big arm around her. "I'll feed you myself if you're too tired to lift your fork."

Our first game was at Galesburg, a fifteen-mile ride on the bus. Resen thought we'd win if Phil Peterson could get through at least five innings of pitching. Rick was his relief and Walt Bedard third in line if the coach got antsy. Robbie told everyone on the bus he used to throw great until he ruined his arm. More big talk.

The booster club had splurged and bought us new uniforms this year. As usual, I came out wearing number one, the smallest size, although one other guy was shorter and fatter. Robbie spent an hour trying on different sizes to make sure he looked good. He liked tight clothes, so his uniform had to be snug. "Samson, no matter what you do, your manhood ain't big enough to show," one kid said. "I'd like to get my uniform before midnight if it's all right."

"Aw, John, nothing's going to look good on you anyway, so what do you care?" Robbie kept shuffling through the pile.

"Get out of there, Samson, you picky woman," Resen yelled.

Robbie continued his quest until he at last had his uniform on. "There," he announced, "and how does the man look?"

"Totally revolting," John said.

"When I look good, I play good," he said, posing.

"Well," I mumbled. "You play *well*."

"Why, thank you, Professor," he said. "Didn't think you'd ever admit it."

Galesburg was the ugliest town I'd ever been to, its claim to fame being a paper mill, an underwear factory and about ten bars. But Galesburg had one big attraction—the dance hall in the middle of town. This was the place my friend Pete wanted to take me to?

"Rick, there she is," I said as we passed the huge building. The parking lot lay empty and littered with papers and cans.

"What *is* that?" Robbie asked. He sat in front of us, engaged in some sort of perpetual motion. Rick had become bus sick and kept his forehead pressed to the window.

"The Galesburg Dance Pavilion," I told Robbie. "My friend meets girls there."

"Now that sounds interesting," he said. "What kind of girls?"

"I don't know, older ones like Pete. If you're underage, you get a red stamp on your hand."

"But you can bring your own," Walt said from across the aisle. "They hardly ever check you."

"You mean you haven't gone?" Robbie asked. "Won't Pete take you?"

"Sure, I just don't want to go."

"You're crazy. Do you think he'd take me?"

"Why don't you ask him?"

The bus pulled up to the Galesburg High School baseball field. We hauled the equipment off the bus and went to warm up. Resen had us stretch, jump around and play catch until it was time to get out on the field.

"You better not screw up," Robbie told me en route to the infield. "Don't forget what I told you."

"You didn't teach me anything," I said, "except not to trust you."

"What's that supposed to mean?" Robbie bounced the baseball hard to me. I grabbed it and sidearmed it to Rick at first. He threw it to Ken and it came back to me.

"It tells you that your motives stink. I could care less who you'd rather not play ball with, since you're such an expert, but if I had known your reason for teaching me, as you put it, I would have quit flat."

"And stayed the stupid chicken that you are."

I picked up the ball and narrowly missed his head with it. Robbie swerved and fell over on his back. "Richardson!" Resen screamed.

I started off the field. Rick hurried over to me. "Can't you wait until after the game?" he said angrily. "You're making a wreck out of me."

Robbie walked up to us. "Professor, sir, I need a minute of your time. Let's waltz across the field, shall we?"

"This playing together on the same team is not going to work," I said as we reached the far corner. "I know you'll be happy about my decision to resign, or should we make it fair—flip a coin, draw straws, pick a number? We just don't get along, Samson. We never did and we never will. I'm sorry for what I did to you, but I didn't understand you and I still don't. Facts are facts. Well, what's it going to be?"

Robbie rested his gloved hand on his hip while the other fidgeted with his hat brim, bright red against his thick black hair. "For God's sake, will you shut up?" he said. "Let's get one thing straight." I looked at the still pink line of the scar I had given him, extending down from his upper lip. "The reason I said I hated McAfree was so you wouldn't owe me, okay? I never hated him. I don't even know him. I figured you'd be good with a little help. The team needed you, that's all. I was doing a job." I heard him breathing hard through his nose. "For sure, you're dumb. And touchy. You always going to be so touchy?"

I shook my head.

"Well then. You have to decide what happens next. I have a rule. I only allow myself to be a punching bag once."

I stood there speechless. Would I ever understand him? He was smart in a way I never will be. Slowly I brought up my right hand. I looked at his face and waited. Then I felt his huge fingers around my thumb and we finished the handshake Robbie had tried two months earlier.

A whoop went up from the other side of the field. We turned to see the East team clapping and whistling, led by Rick, their cheerleader.

"Bunch of damn voyeurs," I mumbled.

Robbie grinned as we walked toward Resen and the others. "Oh, one more thing," he said, stopping.

"What?"

"If you so much as lay one finger on me again, I'll break that neck, the one holding up your brainy head . . . understand?"

We won our first game ten-zip.

Chapter
16

Getting to know Robbie wasn't easy. He had more moods than A & L had car parts. At first neither of us talked to the other without wising off. Sometimes whole conversations were built around who could outdo the other with insults. In the cafeteria the hour went fast because of the cracks traveling between the serving line and the dish room.

Once we traded, me washing, Robbie serving. I left behind a dead fly in the mashed potatoes which Robbie served to Greta Wilkes, the snottiest girl in the school. People from the nearest farm must have heard her shrieks. Another time Robbie squirted shaving cream on the gingerbread and handed those pieces to some guys he wasn't particularly fond of.

Diane was thrilled that Robbie and I were getting along. She was still crazy over him. What made him attractive to girls, anyway? Others besides Diane and

Kelly hung around him, touching and pulling him as if he were some kind of try-me sample. He wasn't the most popular guy ever to hit East, but he fit in pretty well. His sense of humor had me laughing like mad inside. He teased but took the same with a shrug. He was a character in his own play, always ready to put on a show. But sometimes he forced it, his smile fading. I began to understand that Robbie was not a happy person and did everything he could to cover it up. What really was going on inside him?

When we played baseball, no two people cooperated more than Robbie and I. I practically killed myself backing him up at short, and he took pants-tearing nose dives and leaps to ensure the success of our well-oiled machine. After each game we discussed our plays over double cheeseburgers, my treat, of course, our post-game talks the only time Rob and I had serious conversation.

Once, after a close contest, he grinned and slapped my back. "Professor, I never thought you'd turn out so good," he said. It was the first time he had ever complimented me. Then he added, "And to think I made you that way."

Grandpa came to every game, yelling and hooting to the disgust of some of the parents from the other teams.

"Can't your dad get to some of our games?" I asked Robbie once.

I saw something foreign come into his eyes. "He's not interested," he said.

"Am I ever going to meet him?"

"I don't know. Maybe sometime. My friends aren't really welcome at my place."

If I hadn't had the team and the games and my friends, life would have been much worse. In bed at night I thought of Dad. I hadn't seen him for a month. He wasn't improving. Mom was skinny. Her clothes hung on her like dishcloths. I wanted the hurt out of her eyes, but I didn't know how to help her.

Grandpa and I did plenty of talking and wondering about Dad until there was nothing left. "I think it'll be a long time for Henry," he said one night. "I worry more about Anne, if you want to know the truth."

Mrs. Callum listened as I plodded through all the hashed-over thoughts in her office a few weeks later. "You should be allowed to visit your father," she said at the end of my hour. "You are mature enough to see him the way he is, and besides, it might help him."

Sunday morning I drove Mom to Fall Hill, thanks to Grandpa's driving lessons. It took over an hour to get to the small town on the edge of Brownstone Lake.

Halfway up a gentle rise outside the town stood a large brick building surrounded by budding maples and furry pines. The place looked like a school, until we drove up to the front. Then I saw the bars on some of the windows and the sign "Fall Hill Mental Facility." Inside we walked down a long hallway past a recreation area until we got to Dad's room. Bright sun shone straight across the floor to where Dad sat in his chair.

"Hank." Mom's voice was soft. "Look who came to see you."

Dad didn't move his eyes, so I stepped in front of him. "Hi," I said. His hands lay limp on his legs. "Dad, can you hear me?" I remembered this movie about a sister trying to get through to her shell-shocked brother. I looked at Mom. "Does he know I'm here?" I whispered. I pulled another chair across the room and sat next to Dad. My mother sat on the bed.

"It's the same every week," she said. "I sit here with him. I don't do anything. He doesn't do anything. The doctors say he's perfectly capable of speaking, except that he won't. He's punishing me for something he thinks I did to him."

"That's crazy talk." My dad shifted in his chair. "He moved," I said.

"Of course he moves, but it doesn't mean anything."

"Why don't you leave me alone?" my dad said.

"He talked!"

"He says that. It's the same as saying nothing."

"Get out. Get ooooooooooout!" His voice was high-pitched, eerie, his body still. "Get out of here. I don't want you. I want to die." He looked straight ahead. I touched his hand, held it. It was cold. I was terrified and knew I'd cry if I didn't get out of there.

"Why don't you walk around outside," Mom said. She got up. "That's why I didn't want you to come here."

For the next two hours I wandered up and down the hills surrounding the hospital, gazing over the beautiful farmlands and expensive homes half-hidden behind trees and low hills, and the still ponds and white fences.

My mother was going to end up in the room next to Dad's if she wasn't careful. All those years since Dad and I had done things together, had really talked or shared. How could we have lived with him and not realized something was very wrong with him, that it wasn't just his involvement with the business?

"What about the agency?" I asked Mom on the way home.

"I'm training with Stan to take over in your dad's place, so of course I have to quit Best's. In two months I'll be doing everything Stan does."

"Why didn't you tell me? I want to help." I glanced at Mom. Her hands were knotted over her stomach. "I know. You didn't want to burden me."

"Do you have any idea what you mean to me?" she asked, beginning to cry.

She's sliding toward the edge, I thought. But what could I really do? Things were jumbled, depressing. If my dad weren't so selfish, he'd pull out of it. Didn't he see what he had done to my mother? And Grandpa. Dad ought to take a good look at his face.

Walt Bedard called when we got home. "Rick and I'll be over in five minutes," he said.

"Wait. I can't go anywhere tonight. I've got—"

"Be ready," he said and hung up.

Chapter
17

"So what are we going to do?" Walt asked.

"I don't know," Rick answered. "What do *you* want to do?"

"For crying out loud, I thought you had a plan." I let out a disgusted sigh. "We have a history test tomorrow, and I've only made it through World War I."

"Forget it," Rick said. "Give the rest of us a break and get a C on a test for once, will you? We're going to pick Robbie up from work. He'll have a good idea. It's a great night. Relax."

Walt drove up to the Lamplighter a few minutes later. Robbie stood outside under the awning.

"I'll get in the back," he said, "but do you mind making one stop? I want to check something out."

"Where to?" Walt asked.

"Ninth and Ash."

I got in the back. Robbie leaned against the truck's cab

as we started to roll. He looked over and grinned. "Big night tonight," he said. "A wedding reception. You should have seen the bride and groom—all over each other."

"Give them a couple of years," I said. "Bet it wears off."

"I know," he said, trying to keep hair from blowing in his eyes.

"Where do you have to go?"

"To see my old man for a few minutes. He works down at Denning's."

"Really? What does he do?"

Robbie stared straight ahead. "Maintenance. He didn't finish high school or anything, so there's not much he's good at."

"My dad didn't go to school either—college, I mean. He worked himself half to death, that's all, and look where it got him."

"Well, at least he's only ruining himself—or trying to . . . never mind." He raised one hand. "Hey, let's do something wild tonight and stop talking about our dads. It's depressing."

I had to agree. Walt slowed down and stuck his head out the window. "This it?"

Robbie nodded and jumped off. "Be right back," he said, starting toward the rear of the Denning building.

Rick walked over to look in the window of a card shop, while Walt opened the hood of his truck and started poking around.

"Know anything about Robbie's father?" I asked Rick.

"Not really. I drove him to his apartment last week for the first time. I saw his dad sitting outside. He looks exactly like Robbie, only much, much older. It's weird."

"Is he, you know, okay? Is he nice?"

"I wouldn't go so far as to say that," Rick said. "He seemed strange to me. He and Robbie whispered to each other, sort of, like they didn't want me in on anything. It made me wonder if . . ."

"If what?" I asked, glancing toward Denning's.

"Oh, I don't know. The guy reminds me of a hood."

"Come on."

"Just my impression. Might not mean anything."

"We shouldn't talk about him, I guess, since he's Robbie's father."

"Yeah. But the two of them—they act funny around each other. Mr. Samson looks, well, hard—the kind who's been through it."

"I think your imagination's got the best of you."

"Something's going on. You can cut the feeling with a knife when those two are together."

"You've only been with both of them once."

"That was enough."

"Maybe Robbie's dad is antisocial. Maybe he didn't like you." I looked toward Denning's again. Ten minutes had passed. "Should we walk back there and get him?" I asked.

"Give him a few more minutes."

We waited another ten minutes. "I'm going back there," I said. "Are you coming?"

Rick and I walked down the alley Robbie had taken

and found the service entrance. I felt uneasy. Rick tried the door and I rang the buzzer, but we got no response.

"What'll we do?" I asked. Rick shrugged.

After standing there a little longer, we gave up on waiting and went back to the truck.

"There's something wrong with the carburetor," Walt said when we were traveling again. "Smell it?"

"I smell something funny," Rick said, "but it isn't the carburetor."

"Where's Samson?" Walt asked, turning onto the next street. "You know what? Hear that noise in the engine? Something is definitely wrong with my poor baby."

"We don't have any idea where Rob is," I said. Then I saw him running down the street and into a bar called the Hot Tomato. "Stop!" I yelled. "There he is. See him?"

Walt almost ran up the curb. "Where?"

"Just let me out," I said, opening the door. I ran to the entrance. A large man stood in the doorway frowning at me.

"What you want, kid?" he asked, blocking my view.

"My friend's in there. I have to talk to him."

"You can't come in here," the man said. "You ain't old enough."

"I know, but he isn't either. I saw him go in."

"You must be mistaken, kid. No one underage gets in this place. I make sure of that."

I turned and looked at Rick and Walt. "What'll we do?" I asked.

"All of you can get out of here," the man said, taking a step toward us. *"Now."*

We went back to the truck.

"That was one big dude," Walt said. "Are you sure Robbie's in there? I didn't see him. What would he be doing in a bar?"

"I don't know," I said as we headed away from the Hot Tomato.

"We should probably keep quiet about this," Rick said. "I don't know what happened, but it's Robbie's business."

Maybe Rick was right. Maybe Robbie and his dad were involved in something illegal. But it didn't make any sense, his disappearing like that when he knew we were waiting for him.

After I got home that night I thought about Rob for a long time. He and his dad had a bad relationship—the only fact I knew for sure. He had told me that.

Richardson, I thought, you'd make a great detective. What is it with Robbie? What is he hiding, if anything? What did he do tonight when he left Denning's? Did you really see him go into that bar?

The next day was strange. Robbie sat alone at a corner table in the cafeteria, and when I tried to join him, he said, "I'm not in any mood to talk. Mind?"

"What happened to you last night?" came out of my mouth before I thought about it.

I could hardly hear his answer. "You don't want to know." He got up with his barely eaten lunch and went to dispose of his tray. His clothes looked slept in. That afternoon he didn't show up for practice.

I decided I wanted to see him. Rick told me where he

lived, so I got on my bike and rode to Canbury, a run-down section of East Powell. Robbie lived at 202 Fremont in a building that looked like an army barracks.

I knocked on the screen door dotted with chipping blue paint. Someone peered at me from behind a window curtain. Then the door opened. Rick was right about Mr. Samson and Robbie looking alike.

"Well?" he said.

"I came to talk to Robbie," I said.

"Not here."

"Is he at work, or—"

"No." He slammed the door.

I turned and started home. Taking a detour, I rode past the high school and the field where Robbie and I had met that icy morning. I got off my bike at the baseball field and walked to the north dugout. A few bubblegum wrappers and hundreds of sunflower seed shells lay around on the dirt floor. On the bench in one dark corner sat Robbie. "Hey," I said, surprised. "I went over to your place." I sat down beside him. He had his elbows on his knees, his chin resting on the palms of his hands. "Things aren't going so well, are they?" I asked. "What happened? Wasn't your dad at work last night?"

"I know you're curious, but I can't talk about it," he said, almost in a whisper. "Man, I am so exhausted."

"Me, too. I stayed up half the night studying for a history test."

"How'd you come out?"

"Ninety-eight percent."

"Figures. So what did you guys end up doing last night?"

"Nothing. Walt was worried about his truck, so he took us home early. Then we thought of having a poker game, but none of us had more than a dollar. Like to play poker?"

Robbie's jaw tightened. "My favorite," he said. He picked up a rock and flung it out onto the field, then kicked viciously at the dirt.

"What's eating you?" I asked.

"I should have stayed with you guys last night," he said. "I figure I'm young once and I want to have some good times."

"What are you talking about?"

"I'm sixteen already, and when I look in the mirror every morning, half of me wishes I had more whiskers and the other half wants to be a little kid with a mother and dad and brothers and sisters."

"But you have fun. You always do."

"It's being with friends that keeps me from going off the wall. I mean it."

"Maybe we can do some things—you know, this summer."

"Maybe." He sighed.

I got up. "Come over to my house. We'll play tapes or talk to Grandpa."

Robbie laughed bitterly. "Wow. Tapes *and* Grandpa. Look, I don't need any pity, Richardson, unless I ask for it, and you'll never see me do that."

"You sure have a lot of pride," I said. "I told you I only

ask friends up to my room, and I said before that Grandpa would like to see you. So don't make a big issue out of it."

I went to get my bike.

"Think you can get me to your house without breaking my neck?" Robbie asked, walking next to me.

"If you make any more stupid remarks, I wouldn't bet on it," I said.

"I'm not betting on much these days," he answered.

Chapter

18

As it turned out, Robbie pedaled me home. I told him he needed to work his skinny legs more, so they'd be as strong as mine. Grandpa had made some cherry pie, which we finished, and after some encouragement, Robbie ate a cheese sandwich and drank nearly a quart of milk. I didn't think he had eaten anything all day except those few bites of spaghetti at lunch. In an hour he began to look better.

I liked the way Grandpa talked to Robbie, making him smile and relax again. Pretty soon we were exchanging stories of childhood diseases, favorite war films and pets, Grandpa waving his arms all over with his descriptions.

Later we went to my room. Robbie went over everything—the trophies, the team pictures, the scrapbooks, the posters. I sat on the bed after putting in a tape, watching him go from one discovery to another.

"Why weren't you at practice today?" I asked. "Resen had a fit."

"I got sick," he said. He looked at me. "You ever drink besides that one time?"

"Not really. Have you?"

"Once or twice, but my stomach can't take it. Before I came here I got stoned all the time, *all* the time."

"On what?"

"Grass, other things."

"I'm sure you know who the freaks are at East. I'm not touching that crap. You still smoke?"

"No, only when we first moved here. I was bored."

"Well, I don't want any of that around me," I said. Robbie laughed. "I'm not kidding. I know someone who almost died from it."

"You can't die from that."

"You can if you're stoned and driving. Anyway, I'm totally against it."

"Yeah, I know. You're the captain of the Salvation Army." Robbie pulled last year's yearbook off my shelf and started to flip through it. "You guys looked like babies," he said. "Hey, here's Kelly. She hasn't changed much."

"No, she's still beautiful."

"Are you still mad at me for being with her?"

"It depends. How much 'with her' do you mean? You're not, well, you know *what* . . . are you?"

Robbie sat down on my rug. "I'll never tell," he said, still studying her picture. "Nah, we're not doing anything. I want to. She doesn't. I mean, she does, but she won't. She says I have to grow up and all that."

"Do you love her?"

"What do you think?"

"I think you do and I do and a dozen other guys at East do."

"Still hard for you to think of her and me, isn't it?" he said. "But what can I do, stay away? She's everything I like in a girl. We won't end up together, though, because I'm not going to get married or anything until I'm around forty. And I don't want children. I wouldn't be able to treat them right."

"Why do you say that?"

Robbie lay back on the rug, then rolled over on his stomach. "I only know how my dad and I get along and that's zilch. And my mother—"

"I heard about that," I said.

"Sometimes I don't want to think about it, but it always comes back to me. Did you ever have something happen to you that you wish you could change?"

"Only about a hundred things," I said.

"It's the same with me. I don't—I can't understand why my mother chose that guy over me. I never knew my dad till the day she told me I had to go live with him. I told her I'd be a good boy and wouldn't cause them any trouble, but one Saturday she put me on a bus and that was it. I saw her once after that."

"God, I can't believe a mother would do that."

"She loved him more. I don't blame her. Mom was so pretty. She's real little. I could lift her up when I was ten. She'd yell for me to put her down. I tried to tell her how I felt, but I never got the right words out. When the bus pulled away, I started to scream and run up and down the aisle. Some lady pulled me into her seat and made me sit in her lap.

"My dad couldn't stand me. He had a lot of girlfriends. One of them—her name was Fran—tried to be friends. She brought me things. Maybe she wanted my dad to marry her. Anyway, she made me miss Mom all over again and I'd cry and Dad got real mad.

"After we left New Jersey my dad had trouble holding jobs. He's still not too good at it. Anyway, about my mom. When I'm a famous ballplayer, I'm going to find her and give her whatever she wants—a car, a house—"

"Don't you know where she lives?"

"No, she sent me a couple of letters and then they stopped. She must have moved and we moved. Guess she decided it was better to be loyal to her husband."

"Not in my book," I said.

"What do you know?" Robbie said. "You've never had people coming after you in the middle of the night, threatening you because of the money you owe them. You've never had a father who was always on the run, who barely notices you until he wants something out of you." I started to open my mouth. "Richardson, you are as naive as they come. Figure it out."

"Is that why you've been seeing Mrs. Callum?" I asked.

Robbie sat up. "How did you know?"

"I saw you going in there one day."

He got up and walked around the room. "I have to talk eventually," he said. "It stays down there for so long, then comes back up like puke. I can never get her out of my mind. Everywhere I live I become good friends with the school psychologist. What if I have brothers and sisters somewhere?"

"You probably do."

"What a shock. I wonder if they're as good-looking as me."

"I've been seeing Mrs. Callum, too," I said.

"You're kidding. Golden boy?"

"She called me in. My grades. My dad. She thought I was on drugs."

Robbie slapped his leg. "That's really funny. Man, talk about the wrong track. What do you think of her? If I'm feeling normal on appointment days, I just sit there and look at her body. Did you ever think how it'd be with someone like her?"

"Yeah, well, I just wonder what it's like, period."

"We should make it our summer goal."

"Mrs. Callum?"

"No, stupid. I mean we should get laid."

"I thought maybe you already had."

"I'm sorry to have to admit it, but there you are. I haven't."

"There's a slight problem. Who's going to cooperate with us?"

"Your friend could take us to one of those dances and fix us up."

I scratched my head, not wanting to sound dumb. "I always thought the first time should be with, well, someone you love a lot."

Robbie punched my arm. "You're the biggest sissy I've ever met. The thing is you need experience before you're with the important one. It's logical."

It sounded logical.

Robbie scrutinized his arms and legs. "I think I should start lifting," he said, "fill out this skeleton. Have any weights?"

"I think we might have some in the cellar. Maybe if I improved my image I'd feel more like making it with someone."

"Now you're talking," Robbie said.

Chapter
19

On the way to school the next morning I thought about what Rob had said. Why would people come after the Samsons for money when it was obvious they didn't have any? Unless something shady was going on. I felt a strange obligation to Robbie now. I guess we were his family. Mom would have been good for him, too, if she hadn't been caught up in her own worries.

Robbie had brought his grade in algebra from failing to a C. He still came to me for help during school. I didn't mind, and I realized that recently we had stopped the put-downs, instead discussing sports, music and our futures.

During lunch, Diane and I talked about our summer plans. Diane was going to her grandparents' in Iowa as usual. I said I'd be at Fall Hill a lot. Robbie sat at the table with us, staring out the window.

"So what are you going to do?" Diane asked, tapping his arm.

He turned to her and laughed. "Well, I have at least a dozen choices," he said, "but I think I've settled on—Switzerland. The place appeals to me somehow."

"What a wit, Samson," I said.

"Yeah." Robbie looked away. Then he got up. "Time for Robert to clean the drains," he said. "I can't believe what Mrs. Chaffey asks of me around here, but being the wonderful, dedicated worker I am, I wouldn't think of giving her another wrinkle."

"No," I said, "you save that for your friends."

He got rid of his tray and disappeared into the dish room. Next year, I decided, there would be no more messing around with the school cafeteria. Lately Rob and I had been talking about the possibility of getting a job together at a restaurant. But for now this would have to do.

After a while it seemed too quiet in the kitchen. I didn't hear Robbie clattering around in there. "Hey Rob," I called, "what are you doing, taking a shower in the washing machine?"

I walked into the dish room. He wasn't anywhere. The knives and forks sat steaming at the end of the belt, waiting to be polished, but Robbie wasn't running the machine. I heard a faint noise, like something strangling. What was it? A moment later Robbie stumbled in and bent over one of the counters, coughing and holding his stomach, his face gray.

"What happened?" I whispered.

Robbie couldn't answer. He coughed until he ralphed. I caught him as he fell. He had both hands over his chest.

"I'm dying," he said. "Tell my mother I love her. I really do. And Kelly."

"Wait. What happened?"

"I was cleaning the drains—and—I must have put—" He coughed furiously.

"You put what?"

"I mixed—Lime a-way with—bleach and it started bubbling—and the fumes—got in my lungs, I guess. I think I'm poisoned."

"Diane!" I screamed. She ran in holding her spatula. When she saw Robbie and the mess, she burst into tears. "Stop that and go get someone—the nurse, the principal, anyone."

By one, Robbie lay in a hospital bed with IVs in both arms. I convinced the staff to let me stay with him. After watching him sleep for two hours, I went into the hall. Robbie's dad hadn't shown up. A doctor went into Robbie's room, and when he came out I followed him.

"He's ingested a great deal of toxic gas," he said, giving me a sharp look. I already knew about the ingestation. Who did he think found him? "If he rests and lets the IVs work, he can go back to school next week, but it'll be a good month before he can engage in physical activity."

"But he's the best second baseman East Powell ever had. We need him for the state tournament."

"To hell with the tournament," the doctor said. "He could have died. Why kids want to experiment and ruin themselves, I'll never know."

"He wasn't doing that. He was cleaning the drains in the cafeteria."

"He must have known what he was doing," the doctor said, "especially if he'd done it before."

What was he saying, that Robbie did it deliberately? I could never believe that. He liked himself too much to do anything so crazy . . . didn't he?

I went back into the room and saw Robbie in the same position, his arms outstretched, the IVs stuck in each one. I lowered myself into the chair.

I guess I fell asleep because suddenly I jolted upright. I wondered when Robbie would wake up. Then he began to struggle and cough. His hands were strapped down because of the tubes, and when his eyes popped open, he looked panicky and his breath came in short spasms. Then he saw me.

"Todd, get me out of here," he said between coughs. His face grew red and his eyes were bloodshot. He began to kick his feet, sending the blankets sailing.

"Hey, wait a minute, Samson. You have to rest. You practically just got here. Come on now." I managed to push his shoulders back toward the pillow, but Robbie shook uncontrollably, his hair damp with sweat.

"I can't stand this—" He broke off, coughing. "Untie me, *please*."

I know I should have called someone, but I undid the straps. "Don't pull out the needles," I warned. "They have to be there."

"Better," he whispered, sinking back into unconsciousness.

That night I told Mom and Grandpa. "He's done for the rest of the season."

"The poor darling," Mom said. "At least he'll be all right."

"He looks bad," I said.

"I want to visit him tonight," Grandpa said.

Robbie seemed better by the time we got there. Grandpa sat right down on Robbie's bed and took his hand until a nurse came in and asked him to use a chair.

His dad still hadn't come to see him.

"Why doesn't Robbie stay with us for a while?" my mother asked when we got home. "He should have someone to care for him."

The following day at school I had to tell about Robbie's accident at least twenty times. Later I talked to Mrs. Callum, who was far more worried about the whole thing than I thought she'd be. "I know you can't say anything, but . . ." I hesitated. "The doctor hinted around that Robbie might have done it on purpose. I don't believe that, do you?"

I didn't like Mrs. Callum's face. "Sometimes it's unconscious," she said. "Then again, it could have been purely accidental." She touched my arm. "I'm glad he has you," she said.

After school I went to the hospital. Robbie's door was closed. Loud arguing came from inside. At first, I was sure Robbie's father was in there, but then I started hearing pieces of the conversation and I knew it couldn't be him.

What was going on? The door opened with a whoosh and Robbie's doctor rushed past me. I walked into the room. Robbie had an agonized look on his face. He sat rod straight on his bed, arms sticking out from his hospital gown like two bony canes. Whatever the doctor said had scared the hell out of him. When he saw me, his expression changed to relief. He smiled.

"Hey, Todd!" He started bouncing around. The needles had been removed. "I got two breakfasts this morning. Tried for three, but they said they didn't want to have to pump my stomach."

"What was—that about?" I pointed to the door.

Robbie looked away. "Oh, nothing. My dad doesn't want to pay, that's all."

Robbie was lying.

"When are they letting you go?"

"This afternoon."

"My mom wondered if you'd like to stay with us a few days."

"Nah, that's all right. I appreciate the offer, but I'll be okay."

"Did Mrs. Callum visit you this morning?"

"Yeah, and Kelly. Someone told her I was dying." He reached for the top of his water jug and began to play catch with it. "Say, I've had a lot of time to think and I have something to tell you."

"You don't have to thank me for saving you," I said.

"That didn't even cross my mind. I was remembering the night when we talked about Kelly. Now that we're friends, I'm going to settle that part." Robbie got out of bed and walked over to the window. "I told her this morning that I wasn't going to go with her anymore."

"You don't have to be so dramatic," I said. "I'll live.

You two can have your grand passions. I'm a man."

Robbie laughed. "Nope," he said, "that's the way I want it."

"What did she say?"

"That I don't love her anymore. I do, but . . ." The top of his water jug sailed into the wastebasket across the room.

"So you're not going with her."

"Right. Well, according to her, she's got plenty of other guys waiting."

"She said that to make you jealous."

"She succeeded."

"You don't have to do this for me. I'm not that sensitive."

"Only like a pile of mush. But it's not for you. I want to be unencumbered—how's that word, Richardson?— when we start going to those dances in Galesburg."

"So you can get laid." Robbie laughed. "Don't you realize you've had a terrible shock to your system? You can't think of that stuff yet. You're not even going to get to play baseball. Did the doctor tell you?"

"If I feel like playing, I will."

"Sure you will, Samson."

Chapter

20

I visited Robbie at home while his dad worked, but he always seemed on edge. Once he had me leave through the back door when he heard his dad drive up. "Someone might be with him," he said.

Robbie talked about his mom that week. "I think about her too much," he said. "I daydream all the time."

"I read a report that says daydreaming is a useful pastime. It helps a person work out his problems."

"Have you read everything about everything?"

"I try."

"Sometimes you can be such a bore, Richardson. Well, I'm going to find her," he said. "She was living in Ohio when she sent me to my dad. Then they moved to Indiana. That's when we lost touch." He looked at me. "Do you think I'm nuts?"

"I hope you find her someday, if that's what you want."

"That's what I want. How's your dad?"

"Nothing's changed. He could be there for the rest of his life."

"He'll get better," Robbie said, "because he knows you want him back."

Playing ball was only half as much fun without Robbie, although he came to the games and sat with Grandpa. He had to quit his jobs and occasionally would have spells of weakness and coughing. I never saw his dad again, and Robbie avoided talking about him. More and more his mother was on his mind.

He parked at our house constantly now, and we spent hours in my room, listening to tapes and talking. I realized that if he had a little more ambition, he could be anything he wanted. Besides having a brain, he understood far more about life and people than I did. He carefully handed bits of his life to me, calculating the result they would have, revealing just enough to produce the desired response. Maybe he'd tell me everything one day, maybe he never would. But I wasn't going to pry. What I did know was that I needed him, too.

Once he asked, "Do you know why I got a job in the cafeteria?"

"To get on my nerves," I said.

"True, but the other reason is so I could eat. I didn't have any money, and there was never much food in the apartment."

"Am I supposed to feel sorry for you?"

"Don't you?"

I laughed.

Another time he said, "Remember that poem I read to Kelly at her birthday party? I copied it out of the back of our lit book."

"I thought it sounded familiar."

We talked constantly about sex during those evenings and weekends. Robbie hadn't experienced much, but he claimed he knew what he was doing.

"There are too many things to remember," I said. "I think I'd better wait until I'm at least twenty-five, so I don't make a fool of myself."

"Oh, come off it, Richardson, you big yellow chicken."

"I don't think a person's manhood is anything to take lightly," I said. "I'm not ready. I'm only sixteen. I've kissed two girls in my life and one of them was on the cheek."

But the more we talked, the more enticing the subject became to me. We started to discuss the dances again, and slowly my courage grew to the point where I was willing to go to one. Robbie talked to Pete and suddenly they were setting a date. Pete even told us we could use his apartment. I was terrified.

School ended June tenth. Robbie had come close to flunking English, and if I hadn't sat up with him half the night before the final, he probably would have. East Powell had made the finals, gone to State and lost by one run. I won't say whose fault it was, but if Rob had been playing, we'd have won for sure.

Diane left June fifteenth. Robbie and I went to see her off. I hugged her. Rob gave her a kiss and told her to get

151

a good tan. She melted. I guess it wasn't my right in life to understand his effect on females.

Now the whole summer waited for Rob, Rick and me. Number one on my list was the sandpit, our swimming hole four miles out on the highway. Kids from all over crowded there. At night Robbie came over for dinner and talked to Grandpa and me. Being with both of them made me feel good, made me forget.

Robbie went to Fall Hill with me one weekend. My dad sat in his chair, completely uncommunicative while I talked to him. Rob sat next to me, joining in and finishing some of my sentences, but even his enthusiasm wore off.

"Man," he said when we got outside, "how can you take it? I'd rather have my dad mad at me than look like a burnout. What a downer."

"Are you still seeing Mrs. Callum?" I asked one night.

"She calls me, can you believe it?"

"She really must like you. You should have seen her the day after your accident. Maybe she loves you."

"Can you blame her?"

My mom was crazy over Robbie. She liked having someone around she could pay special attention to. Robbie lapped it up but flattered her so much that I got him aside one day and told him not to lay it on so thick. "The way you talk, someone might think she was Miss America," I said. "Don't give her any hope. There isn't any."

"Hey," Rob said, "she's beautiful to me. I hope my mom's like that when I find her."

Pete mentioned the dances several times. He wanted

to fix us up. I told him I didn't want anyone too old. It might look funny. Pete acted hurt. "I'm not that ancient, am I?" he asked. "The girls I date are only nineteen or twenty."

"That's too old," I said.

"When are you going to loosen up?" Robbie asked. "Man, you're some kind of iron pants."

"We can find our own girls," I said. "Pete, didn't you tell us we could do anything we set our minds to?"

"Well, when you do, my apartment's available."

"You're great," Robbie said, shaking his hand.

"You haven't seen his apartment," I said, coughing.

"Professor, remember, we're like brothers. What one does, the other does. Are you ready for the ultimate in the life of a man?"

"If that's what it is and that's what we are, then I guess so," I said.

Chapter

21

"I've been thinking," I said.

"Congratulations."

Rob and I had spent the afternoon doing yard work to pick up some extra money for Galesburg, and then had collapsed in my room with the shades drawn. The heat was unbearable.

I wiped my face with my shirt, then sat up and pulled it off.

"No, really," I said. "Before your cafeteria accident you worked two jobs."

Rob picked up my shirt and threw it at me. "Brilliant. Have any other sharp observations?"

I scratched my head. "You must have made decent money. What did you do with it?"

"Is that any of your business?"

"Well, no, but didn't you think of saving any of it for Galesburg? You talked about the place enough."

"Kelly and I went out a lot. Women are expensive."

"You didn't do all that much. After basketball practices, baseball and work, how much time did you have left for Kelly?"

Robbie grinned. "Kept track of us, huh?"

I felt myself turning red. Had he guessed? "Shut up," I said. Both of us were practically asleep. Rob sat propped against the foot of my bed, the light from under the window shade cutting across his body onto mine, which was sprawled across the bumpy rag rug. "You never had any money, come to think of it. You always borrowed when we went out, at least most of the time."

"I helped at home with food, okay?" He slid to the floor, out of sight. "What's the difference, anyway?"

I smelled both of us in the closed, dark room. My head began to hurt. I always get nasty when my head hurts. "Food? You told me there was hardly ever any food at your place." I got up and turned on the bed light and slid a tape into the player. A guitar wailed through our silence. I looked at him. "You'll have to make your story better than that," I said.

"Meaning?"

"Meaning nothing fits. You earned money, but you never had any. Then you told me people came after your dad for money. Why? I've seen your apartment, remember? Nothing you have in there could have cost much, if you'll pardon me for saying so. What could you possibly owe someone?"

"You ask too many questions."

"I'm not trying to be nosy. It's just—"

"The hell you aren't, Richardson. Drop it."

"Something's wrong," I said. "I think I know what it is. I want to help, that's all."

Robbie looked at the ceiling, then at me. He got up and sat on my bed. "Why don't you put something else on?" he said. "Some heavy metal. This reeks."

"You do it. I'm taking a shower. Or do you want to go first?"

He shook his head and started to flip through the tapes.

I walked to the bathroom door. Then I turned. "It's illegal, isn't it?" I said. He didn't move. "I mean, I wouldn't think less of you if you had to—do something like that to survive."

Robbie's head jerked up. "Is that what you've thought all this time?" He laughed. "That I'm a thief—or—or dealing drugs? I can't believe it."

"Then what is it? Can't you stop the game playing? It's tearing you up." He put his head down and began looking through the tapes again. "Guess I'll take my shower," I said.

As the water washed over me, I became more confused. Whatever trouble Rob had must be between his dad and him. A private matter, I told myself, so, Richardson, stop bugging him.

I walked out of the bathroom with a towel wrapped around my waist, feeling small for having thrown the conversation at him. He lay motionless on my bed, staring at the ceiling. A shadow covered his face. "You're going to sweat all over my bed," I said. I walked over to him. "I'm sorry—for thinking the worst." His eyes remained fixed. "It's because of the night you disappeared. I saw you go into that bar—by accident. We weren't following you—and when I went to the door, this big guy denied you were there."

"That was Charlie. Of course he's not going to tell you I'm inside. None of them wants the cops down his throat." He chewed on one of his knuckles. "If you saw me, I understand why you thought what you did."

"Yeah, well." I grabbed for something to say. "You hungry or something? I'll go fix us a sandwich."

Robbie dropped one leg over the bed. He still didn't look at me. "All right. I should have told you everything a long time ago," he said, "but . . . man, I'm so ashamed of the whole thing. It's a mess."

"Well, if it's about your dad, I know how you feel, at least a little. I get frustrated about mine all the time. I wonder what I did, what I can do to help."

Robbie turned over and looked at me. "There's nothing that's going to help my dad and me," he said. "We're in a trap, both of us, and we can't get out."

I didn't say anything. I waited. Robbie let out a huge sigh, the expression on his face becoming one I'd never seen before. Gone was the ego. Gone was the courage he showed when he played ball. Gone was the mischief and the humor. I saw something scared and open, as if he had cut himself in two, letting me see the side he had never shown anyone.

"I want to tell you," he whispered. "I've wanted to for a long time, but . . ."

"You don't have to. I don't care." I walked to the window and pulled up the shade. The afternoon had begun to cool off and I could smell the thick grass and the lilies of the valley below.

"Why do people come after us for money? Take a guess." Rob stood beside me.

"I *have*. I don't know."

"My dad, he has an addiction. It's not anything physical. It's something he's done ever since I've lived with him. He gambles."

"He's a professional gambler, like—Las Vegas? Atlantic City?"

"Nah, he does it in slimy back rooms, guys' apartments, in warehouses, bars. He gambles what he has on him, what I have on me. He gambles if we're broke. If he wins, he gambles it away. If he loses, they come after him, take what they can, threaten us, and if the debt is too big, we run. I haven't told you half the places I've lived. Or the parts of town. Or the scum my dad hangs around with."

"Is that what your dad was doing in the Hot Tomato?" Rob nodded. "But why did *you* go there?"

"Why do you think?"

"He wanted your money?"

"When I saw he wasn't at work that night, I knew where to look, but I didn't want you guys to know. I always worry when he starts a streak of this stuff. He's gotten beat up before.

"Sure he wants my money. Sometimes I get to keep it if I can find a good hiding place. But most of the time he either demands it or begs for it, promises he's going to quit if he wins big. He really believes it. I used to. Like the time he did win and he said, 'We're going out to paint the town red. I'm getting you something nice, and then we'll go on a trip. Want to visit your mother?' Told me that over the phone. By the time he got home—at three the next morning—he was broke again. He takes chances on everything. He'd bet on how fast an ice cube melts if he thought he could make a few bucks on it."

"Wait a minute." I tried to remember. "I don't get it. You told me you don't know where your mother is, right? So why did your dad—"

"*He* knows."

I walked away from Rob, trying to get my brain to make some connections. "If *he* knows, why don't *you* know?"

"Let me go back five years. I guess my mother felt guilty about shipping me off. She used to send money for me, and my dad told me he put it aside somewhere. I didn't realize the trouble he was in then. I only knew I spent a lot of time at night by myself, and in the morning my dad either whistled or cussed. Of course, he never kept the money for me."

"But didn't your mom know he was a—"

"I don't think so. After a while, when I was older, the money stopped, or so he said. But then he'd ask sometimes if I wanted to see her. It confused me. I'd get excited and hopeful and the next thing we'd be running again, only I didn't know why yet. Then one day I found a money order in an envelope addressed by my mom. I knew her handwriting. It slanted way to the left. No return address. I got very upset. Fifty dollars. She figured I was worth fifty dollars. I thought of fancy bikes and hot fudge sundaes. She'd been sending my dad money for me all along, and he had spent it and let me think she didn't care about me anymore."

"Did she ever write?"

"Maybe. I never saw a letter, though."

"But how did she send money if you moved all the time?"

"I'm sure my old man let her know where we were. I was thirteen when I found the envelope and asked about it."

"What did he say?"

Robbie sank down on the rug. "He said it was none of my business, and if I ever mentioned it again, he wouldn't let me see her. That kept me quiet. What I didn't realize is that he didn't intend to anyway. He only baited me with her to make sure I'd stay."

"And when you started working?"

"I had to give it to him, most of it, just to keep him out of trouble."

I thought of Robbie asking me if I knew of a job opening somewhere. I thought of the sweater without a shirt, the pathetic clothes he wore, the night he told us he hoped to stay in East Powell. The reason hadn't been Kelly at all.

"How can you live with him?" I asked, my voice sounding unnaturally loud.

"I'm the only one he's got."

160

"But after everything he did to you? What he kept from you?"

"I know he doesn't care much about me," Robbie said, laughing a little. "He won't talk to me about school or my friends. If I didn't buy my own food, I could starve and he wouldn't notice. But I'm saving up. I hide what money I can—I've got a good place—and someday I'm taking it and going to find my mother."

I saw him that first night he ate dinner with us, his mouth stuffed with meat loaf, smiling at my mom, thanking her. I saw the twenty-dollar bill floating to the floor. How had he managed to salvage that much? Was that money part of what he had hidden for his secret mission?

"Winning is all he thinks of, the only thing that matters to him. Finishing high school here is all that matters to me. I want it so bad, but I never know what's going to happen next. Most people want to stand out, be different, you know? Honest to God, I just want to be like everyone else."

Robbie put his head in his hands. "That night I went to the Hot Tomato my dad was in trouble again. He already owed one guy three thousand dollars before, and in this game he was behind by five hundred. I get this panicked feeling and I say, 'Come on, Dad, stop now, okay?' I give him all the money I have on me—my tips. He doesn't answer. Then two men come in from the back and grab me and shove me around, and while one holds me, the others get my dad down and start hitting him. 'Want to see your dad die, kid?' this ugly guy asks me. 'Better tell him to pay up.' My dad pukes all over the floor. 'Your kid's gonna get it, too, man,' another one says, and I feel this arm around my neck, squeezing all the air out."

My mouth had gone dry. I felt my heart thudding hard against my ribs. "What did you do then?"

"They let us go. I knew they would. They wanted money. But that night I wished with everything I had . . . I wished . . ." Robbie began to shake. He closed his eyes tight and let himself backward onto the rug. "I wished they *would* have killed him. I wanted him dead. I know it's wrong, but I wanted to be free."

A long painful something was working its way through my body that wouldn't let me breathe. It caught at my throat, making my words come out funny.

"You—someone's got to do something. Have you told Mrs. Callum all of this?"

"She knows about the gambling, nothing else. She's tried to talk to him. It doesn't do any good." He sat up and ran his hands through his hair.

"Maybe you should tell her everything. Maybe Grandpa could help with the debt. Maybe—"

Robbie stood up and stepped in front of me. "It's my problem," he said. Then he gave me a puzzled look. "You're crying," he said softly. He touched my arm. "You're a good friend."

I wiped my eyes. "What are you going to do?" I asked. "Did your dad raise the money?"

"Yes, but I don't know how. I don't know what to do anymore. This isn't the end. It's just going to start all over again. No one can help. There's nothing anyone can do."

Chapter
22

We weren't exactly in the mood to talk about Galesburg that night, so Robbie decided to go home. The air sat thick with my questions. What I had to digest I wasn't sure I could handle. Reasons for all his previous behavior were obvious now. How many opportunities would he miss because of his father's lack of control?

Knowing about Robbie changed things that night. Why hadn't he asked for help? He had to do it alone, play his lonely game. The day I beat him up was an anthill compared to the tension he'd been living with. And what about the cafeteria accident? Is that what it was?

Sometime after ten I went downstairs to find something to eat. I had been lying on the bed listening to the tapes without really hearing anything. I had even tried to imagine what it would feel like having my father threatened in front of me.

"Hi," I said.

My mother looked up and smiled. "Todd, have you read the sports page? It says here Rick was nominated to the all-state team as a sophomore."

"I know. He'll get a lot of offers by the time he's a senior."

"I haven't seen him lately."

"He's working at the Dairy Queen."

"Well, maybe I'll get a chance to congratulate him sometime."

When I talked to her these days, she'd always stare at her fingernails as if they were the most important part of her body, examining them, biting them. She got up and folded the paper. "Morning comes too early. Keep the music down, okay?"

"Sure, Mom. Say, Mom?" I went over to her, kissing her quickly on the cheek. "I love you," I said, taking off before she could say anything.

I didn't see Robbie the next day. Rick and I went to the sandpit.

"Thought you and Robbie were working," Rick said on the way. "What's he doing?"

"I don't know."

"Why didn't you call him?"

"I just didn't, all right?"

"What's the matter?"

"Nothing. My head feels like a lead pipe, that's all."

The sandpit was crawling. I surveyed the total scene. People lay body to body all over the sand and bobbed head to head in the water. Among the mob I spotted

Kelly on a pink towel back near the big sand hill. She had three guys surrounding her. I realized I hadn't thought about her for weeks. I guess it was the lack of the painful twinge I used to get. Smiling to myself, I decided to say hello and act cool toward her.

Rick went to the diving area, I headed for the pink towel. Kelly was wearing a bikini that barely covered anything, and when she saw me she sat up, squinting. She nearly fell out of her top. I didn't want to stare, but my eyes wouldn't look away.

"Hi, Todd!" she said. "What have you been up to?"

"Oh, nothing much. Rob and I are doing yard work to pick up a few extra bucks."

"How is Robbie?" She was trying to keep her voice normal. "What else have you two been up to?" She picked up a handful of sand and played with it. "You know, I should be furious with you," she said flatly. "He's with you all the time now. But we'll get together again. I know we will."

"Probably." She gave me an anxious look. "We've been going to those dances in Galesburg," I lied.

"Sit down," she said, patting the towel. Her groupies got up and left. I obeyed and she smiled, her dimples deep in her tanned face. She shook her hair back and put her hand on my shoulder. The old familiar ache grabbed at my stomach, and with her so close in her bikini I began to feel giddy.

"I've missed you," Kelly said. "Would you like some of my suntan lotion?" I nodded. Reaching into her bag, she brought out a brown tube, uncapped it and rubbed some cream on my back and over my shoulders. "I've always wanted to go to one of those out-of-towners," she said.

I turned to her. "Would you like to go with me?"

Kelly sighed. "My dad might not let me. You know."

"Does he hate me?"

"No, but he doesn't trust kid drivers."

"We're going with Pete. He's older."

"Are you sure?"

"Oh yes," I said, nodding my head like a charging goat. "Want to?" Oh God, I prayed, let her say yes.

"Does Robbie take a date, usually?"

So that was it. "You want Robbie to take you," I said.

"No, I'd like to go with you. I just wondered, that's all." Bending toward me, she kissed my cheek. I wanted to climb all over her. What was wrong with me? Not three minutes ago I thought I was cured. I'd have to sit on my hands if she did anything else.

"I don't know when we're going again. We don't take dates. We meet girls out there. So I'll call you."

"I'd like that," she said, lying back down.

I looked at every part of her again and knew it was time to go swimming. On one hand I was so happy I wanted to jump all over the sand, but on the other I knew Kelly only wanted to be near Robbie. She wasn't interested in me at all, only in getting Robbie any way she could. Fool that I was, I wanted to be around Kelly for any reason, even if it meant sharing her with Robbie.

"Bye, Kelly," I said.

"See you." She sounded sleepy. I took one last look and left her.

Robbie was sitting on our porch when I got home. I felt shy riding up to him. We sat for a while, watching cars pass. The sun disappeared behind and reemerged from the clouds, like lights dimming and being turned up again.

"I saw Kelly," I said. "I asked her to go to the dance in Galesburg with us. She's still in love with you."

"What did you do a dumb thing like that for?"

"Because of her orange bikini."

"Kelly's not the kind of girl you want to experiment with. She's the kind you want to end up with, if you're lucky."

"Well, I'm not planning on trying anything."

"Exactly. You can take her some other time. You sure got sunburned today."

"I know. It hurts."

"If anyone ever looked ugly with a sunburn, it's you."

"Hey, if my legs were as long as yours, I'd blow you off the map with my body and the girls would totally ignore you. You would cease to exist."

"So you agree that I'm light-years ahead of you. If you watch carefully, Richardson, you might learn something. Even then, all you'd get in girls would be my discards. They'd only want you if there wasn't a chance with me."

"I have analyzed you, Samson," I said, "and have finally come to an intelligent conclusion as to what you're made of inside."

"What, Professor?"

"Bullshit."

Chapter
23

Pete had a girlfriend named Meryl, and she had two friends, Leeann and Deborah. Pete wanted us to meet the girls the next Friday at the pavilion in Galesburg, then take them back to his apartment. Robbie and I still had thoughts of finding our own girls, but Pete assured us Leeann and Deborah were very nice and we'd have a wonderful time.

When Friday arrived, Robbie and I were excited. Robbie bounced around grinning; I sat still and let the butterflies take over. I told Mom and Grandpa that I might be spending the night at Pete's. Robbie didn't have to tell his dad anything, since his whereabouts were never questioned.

Friday afternoon Robbie bought himself a pair of pants and an oxford cloth shirt, both of which fit like the rest of his stuff—tight. He got dressed at my house, spending nearly forty minutes on his hair. He offered to fix mine, but I told him a five-minute fluff job was enough for me, since I didn't care to speed my balding process.

"Would you look at that. Damn!" he said from my bathroom. "A zit."

"Leave it alone," I said. "You'll make it worse."

"Richardson, you're going to make someone a wonderful mother someday."

"Come on," I said. "I heard Pete drive up."

We went downstairs. Grandpa and Mom were talking to Pete. "You have to be the most handsome young men I've ever seen," my mother said when she saw us. She gave both of us a hug and kiss. Robbie turned red.

"The girls are in for a real treat tonight," Grandpa said, chuckling.

"Oh, wait," Mom said. "Let me get your picture." Mom took terrible pictures. They turned out with the human part in one corner and a tree in the middle. She ran to get her camera.

"You'll be glad I took it," she said as we posed.

It wasn't until recently that I realized how right she was.

Chapter
24

There must have been two hundred cars parked on the streets surrounding the pavilion. I wondered on the way whether I had put on enough deodorant. I glanced at my shirt. Maybe I wasn't dressed right. Did I look too young? Would Leeann be short enough?

Rob kept wiping his hands on his pants until I told him he was going to get them dirty. Pete couldn't stop talking about the girls we were going to meet. I wasn't sure I wanted to meet anyone.

Inside, the dance floor rested between two bar areas, one for mixed drinks, the other nonalcoholic, which Robbie and I went for right away to remedy our dry-mouth syndrome. There was a huge dance area with a bandstand in the middle. The building was crowded.

"Let's watch," Robbie said, "see if any good ones pass by."

A girl about our age was staring at Robbie from a nearby table. He noticed and smiled. They glanced back

nd forth at each other for two band numbers. Finally
he came over and asked Rob to dance. She had long
uuburn hair that hung to her waist. When Robbie came
>ack, he said, "Isn't she gorgeous? Too bad it wasn't a
low one. Think of what I could have got my hands on."

"What's her name?"

"I don't know. We didn't talk."

"*You* didn't talk? Impossible."

"I couldn't think of a thing to say."

The girl had gone back to her table and was staring at
Robbie again. We stood in the same spot for another ten
minutes, watching the girl turn down two other guys, all
he time keeping her eyes fixed on Rob.

"Here's a slow one," I said. "Go ask her."

"Nah."

"What's all this bull you've been giving me about your
bility with women? You're worse than I am."

"I don't see you asking anybody."

"It's just that you've been looking forward to tonight
or weeks, and now that we're here, it's like you're
cared or something."

The girl walked over again, smiling. "Well?" she said.
Ie nodded and took her hand. The band was playing a
omantic song. Robbie was going to get his wish. They
nelted into the crowd, rotating mirror balls overhead
preading a speckled blanket around the room.

"They're here," Pete said behind me. "I've got us a
ble. Where's Robbie?"

"Dancing. Look, do I have to go through with this
.eeann thing?"

"Just come and meet her. If you don't like her, we can work out something."

"How old did you say they were?"

"Leeann's nineteen and Deborah's eighteen. Not too bad, is it?"

"I still can't figure out why they'd want to be with guys our age." Pete didn't answer me and I immediately became suspicious. He waved to Robbie.

"Did you talk to her?" I asked Rob when he joined us.

He grinned. "No, but the body language was great."

Pete took us to the other side of the building where three girls sat, all appearing far too womanly for either Robbie or me. I was so nervous I even had sweaty feet. Pete motioned us to the chairs and sat down beside Meryl, a woman with huge breasts and a tiny nose.

"Robbie, meet Deborah. Todd, Leeann. Robbie and Todd, Meryl."

Robbie suddenly became Mr. Charm. "Nice to meet you," he told the girls, shaking their hands. Deborah seemed taken by his smooth manner. This lady didn't know it yet, but she was sunk. I could see the dashing lover look come over his face, the one that got them all, from Mrs. Chaffey to my mother.

My date disappointed me. Her face was all right, but her hair looked like a Brillo pad and she was skinny, though shorter than I, a real contrast to Deborah, who had a delicate look like a ballerina. How had Pete got such a pretty girl to go out with a sixteen-year-old boy, especially one who planned to enlist her help for something very touchy?

"Did you pay those women or what?" I asked Pete in the washroom. "I know you did something."

"I promised to fix their cars," he said, digging into one of his pockets. "Did you remember to pick up some of these?" He held out a box of Trojans. "I didn't think it was tactful to ask if either is on the Pill."

"Oh my gosh," I said as he pressed some into my hand.

"As they say, don't let a little thing you poked in fun screw you up for the rest of your life."

I could just imagine trying to find the nerve to buy something like that. "Well, thanks," I said, stuffing them into my pocket.

By midnight I was having a blast. Leeann was a crack-up, and even if she thought I was too young for her, she didn't show it. "Go dance with some other girls if you want," she said. "There are some real cute ones here." But I really liked her, and she was a great dancer besides.

When it was time to leave, Pete suggested we go to Bernie's Bowl. He might have picked a better place, but nobody objected. Robbie was so enthralled with Deborah that I doubt if he even knew he had climbed into her car. At Bernie's he fastened his eyes on different sections of her anatomy while eating his hamburger, a lopsided grin on his face.

By twelve-thirty we were at Pete's apartment, and, as I expected, it looked terrible. His bed rested against one wall in the living room, a dirty fake-fur cover pulled carelessly over the top. Papers, books and magazines lay next to the bed along with half-filled glasses. At the opposite end of the room he had a set of shelves made with boards and cement blocks, on which was his stereo. The girls took little notice, and Robbie jogged around from room to room—there were only three—ending up in the bathroom. Pete offered the girls some beer.

"Meryl and I are going back out," he told us. "There's plenty to drink in the fridge, so have fun."

Robbie went over to the stereo and put on some of Pete's music, which was so bad it even made me jittery. Leeann got herself a beer. What was I doing here? Up to now the evening had been great. We could have ended it. I wondered where Pete's deodorant was. With his sense of organization, I'd probably find it under his pillow. To think Rob and I might be here all night. How many times could a guy do it in one night?

Leeann came over and put her arm around my shoulders. Her breath smelled like beer and her frizzled hair brushed against my neck. Despite the fact that I didn't much care for her looks, she began to have an effect on me.

Deborah took off the jacket she was wearing over a strapless top while giving Rob a sweet smile, then a kiss on his cheek. He looked like he wanted to devour her, but all he did was smile.

"Don't you want a beer, too, honey?" Leeann asked, still hanging on my arm.

Honey? "Not right now. I'm not used to beer." I sounded like a baby.

Leeann rubbed my cheek. *No, no whiskers yet.* "How old are you, Todd?"

"Sixteen last November."

She smiled. "I love boys like you," she said, "so sweet and sexy."

From across the room Robbie laughed hilariously. My face must have turned as red as a bullfighter's cape. "I don't know what you mean," I mumbled, breaking away from her.

"Oh, don't be offended," she said softly. "You're very cute and I like being with you."

"Well . . . thanks. I was going to ask, how old are you?"

"Twenty-three. Why?"

"Twenty-three!" Robbie yelled.

"What are you, Samson, an echo?" I said. Under my breath I said, "Twenty-three, that liar Pete."

Leeann put her hands on my chest. "Well, don't you want to kiss me?" she asked, her eyes getting that smoldering look.

"Uh, yes, but I haven't, you know—I don't—"

"What do you think I'm here for?" Leeann put her hands on her hips in a dare, but I felt as though someone had just slapped plaster all over me and it had hardened.

"I think I'll get a Coke or something," I said. "My throat's awfully dry."

Leeann dropped her arms, sighing. "Get me a beer while you're at it," she said.

Deborah was kissing Robbie's neck. How could I get past them into the kitchen? I looked at Leeann and shrugged.

The beat of the music filled the room with a soft, easy pulse, since Rob had found something decent to play. Robbie and Deborah began to move with the music, their mouths fused together. I stood mesmerized, watching Robbie get inside Deborah's elastic top while she unbuttoned his shirt and put her hands inside. Then suddenly Robbie froze and stepped slowly away from Deborah. He rebuttoned his shirt, smiling an apology to everyone. Don't stop now, I said silently. Go for it, Rob.

"Think I'll get a beer," he said. Deborah adjusted her top.

Rob plopped down on Pete's bed. Deborah lay down beside him. "Maybe it's time to split up," she said. "Why don't you guys go in there?"

Leeann glanced at me. "Want to?" she asked.

What I really wanted was to stay and watch Robbie to see what I should do, but Leeann pulled me away. What we entered was Pete's junk room. By comparison, his living room looked like a palace. Leeann went to the day bed in the corner, then beckoned me to follow. We sat on a pink-and-purple quilt.

She took my face in her hands and kissed me, pushing her tongue in at the same time. She stroked my back and chest and something else besides. Not only was I completely mindless, but I could have made out with a gorilla at that point and still been horny.

Then it was my turn with shaking hands to touch what she guided my hands to feel. Pushing me on my back, she climbed on top, stretching herself over me like a cat. I started breathing funny. At first, I thought it was because Leeann was on top of me, but she didn't seem that heavy. Then I knew something wasn't right. I couldn't stop panting, and it had nothing to do with sex. Well, maybe it did at first, but by this time panic had set in and I sat up, practically tossing Leeann on the floor.

"Honey, baby, what's wrong?" Leeann cried, peering at my hyperventilating body through the hair that drooped over her eyes.

I wiped sweat off my nose and attempted to calm myself. "I'm one of those guys," I gasped, "who can't seem—to handle excitement. Gosh, I wish I knew."

A full ten minutes later I finally began taking normal breaths. Leeann patted my arm constantly and asked if I'd be all right. "I thought you wanted this night," she said, mussing my hair.

I shook my head. "I don't know . . . I guess I'm not ready." I kept my eyes on a box of dirty rags by the closet.

"But Pete told me—"

"Yeah, I know, but I never really went along with it."

"That's okay, darlin'."

"I've always thought that the first time should be with someone you love. Not that I don't like you a lot because I do. You've been nice to me. But there's been this girl I'll probably love for a long time. It's just her right now. Can you understand?"

"I wish someone loved me like that." She fixed her hair. "You're different from Pete. You know what you want."

"Maybe I'm just dumb."

"Huh-uh. I know a smart guy when I see one." She gave my cheek a friendly pinch. "What's your friend out there like? He's cute."

"He's to blame for tonight. He's very experienced already—in his mind. Get it?"

Leeann giggled. "All the know-how but no partner, huh? The little devil."

"I'm sure he'll be an expert before the night's over. He

177

has an effect on women. I just wish *I* knew what it was."

"Yes," Leeann agreed, "I can see it. He's appealing, the kind of guy you want to take home with you and feed. Know what I mean?"

"My mother does," I said.

"You don't need to worry. When your time comes, you'll be a great lover. You really turned me on."

"I did?"

"You bet." I had to smile. "Say," she said, "we have most of the night ahead of us and we can't walk in on the other two, so . . ." She thought for a moment. "Why don't we crash? I don't know about you, but I'm pooped. We'll both fit here, and it'd be nice sleeping next to you. You're really a good-looking guy, you know?"

"Thanks," I said shyly. I wanted to thank her for understanding, too, but I didn't know how. As Leeann and I got comfortable, I thought about the night. I heard Leeann start to snore, and then I fell asleep.

Robbie shook my shoulder. I opened my eyes. It was still dark. "Man, you must have had some workout," he whispered. "Deborah wants to leave. Can you wake up Leeann?"

"Sure." I yawned. "What are we going to do?"

"Go back to sleep or walk home. It isn't too far."

I woke Leeann, who staggered to the bathroom, then joined Deborah, still as pretty as when we first saw her at the dance. We said good-bye to the girls. Leeann winked at me and blew a kiss. Deborah smiled at Robbie.

We decided to walk home. We'd had enough of Pete's apartment. After a couple of salami sandwiches apiece, we locked up and left.

Chapter
25

"How was it tonight?" Robbie asked after we had gone a block.

"Good," I said. "Leeann was pretty nice. How about Deborah?"

"We really hit it off."

"I noticed. So tell me, was it the way you thought it would be?"

Robbie whistled. "Exactly and better. I can't wait to do it again. Deborah was proud she gave me a good time. *She's* twenty-four."

"Pete's a real buzzard," I said to myself.

We walked two city blocks as Robbie described his adventure in detail. Then he stopped. "What's the matter, Professor? Were you disappointed or something?"

"No," I said. "I just didn't do it."

"Didn't do what?"

"I didn't do IT. I decided not to."

Robbie's jaw dropped. "Why?"

"I don't know. Maybe I still feel the same as when we first started talking about tonight. It's got to be that way for me." I expected Robbie to hand me a lecture on the evils of being a prude, but he didn't. In fact, he didn't say anything for a long time.

"Want to spend the night?" I asked after a while. "As long as you don't mind, I'd like to hear it all again for future reference."

"I'd better go home. I'm tired. I gotta sleep."

"I guess! Well, call me when you get up," I said. "Grandpa's barbecuing steaks tomorrow."

"Great. I'll be there," Robbie said, grinning.

We reached out dividing point, said good-bye and started home in different directions.

I couldn't believe the clock said three when I finally propped myself up the next afternoon. I got something to eat, then tried calling Rob. No answer. Maybe he was still sleeping. The one time he stayed over at our house he had watched an old war movie until four in the morning and slept until dinnertime. I tried again at five and six, then told Grandpa to put on one less steak.

Sunday I stayed home while Grandpa and Mom went to Fall Hill. I called Robbie's place again, and when I still got no answer I hopped on my bike and rode to the apartment in Canbury. As I approached the building my stomach twisted. Both the inside and screen doors were wide open, the interior a dark, gaping hole.

"No!" I shouted, jumping off my bike. I ran to the door. "Hello?" I called. "Rob? You in there?"

I heard steps on the gravel behind me. I turned. "They're gone," a woman said. She dragged one arm across her forehead. "Hot today, isn't it?"

"Where did they go?"

"You a friend of theirs?"

"Robbie's."

"Oh yes, what a nice boy. He always helped me carry out my trash. I'm the landlady. The way some people just up and leave. The boy's father owed me rent money, too. You should see what they left in there. Everything. Go on in. Go ahead."

I walked into the dark living room. The woman followed me. A chair had been knocked over. There was broken glass in the kitchen, papers everywhere. I looked around. "Damn," I said.

"Something strange was going on around here, I'm sure. Saw a couple of characters sneaking here and there, but you see everything in neighborhoods like this. I suppose you know more than I do about the Samsons."

I shrugged and went back outside. "He didn't even realize it," I mumbled. "He didn't even care."

"What, dear?"

I bent and picked up a scrap of paper near the door. "That his son was the best second baseman East Powell High ever had. And that's saying a lot."

"That's too bad," she said in a soothing voice. "I'll bet you'll miss him, too. Such a sweet boy. I don't believe they'll be coming back."

I went to my bike, taking a long time to pedal back home. Halfway there I opened my hand and looked at the damp, wrinkled piece of paper and smiled. "Call me sometime," it said. "Leeann—555-6258."

I sat in the den until it got dark. I wondered where Rob and his dad were hiding. I hoped he'd call, tell me that he was all right. Or maybe he'd show up in a few days and Mom would insist that he come to live with us. I planned how we'd change my room to accommodate another bed.

I decided not to worry Grandpa and Mom about Robbie, but after a week Grandpa started asking where he was, and Mom wanted him to sample her new chicken recipe. Another week went by, and I knew I had to tell them. "Robbie's gone," I said. Grandpa sat down. His face had kind of a destroyed look.

"Was it that bad for him?" he asked, hurt filling his eyes.

"Yes. I'll tell you all about it sometime, but I can't just now."

For the first two weeks after Robbie left I couldn't find anything interesting to do. I never realized how much I depended on him. Kelly. I'd have to tell her.

"Shit," Rick said over a chocolate-dipped cone at the DQ. "He could have called one of us. Well, we're back to you and me again, old buddy."

"I'm going to start looking for a job," I said.

"I'm really going to miss Robbie," Rick said. "Know what he told me? That you, your mom and your grandpa were the best people he ever met. Maybe I was right after all about his dad. We'll never know, will we?"

I shook my head.

Most of the time I lay around and watched TV or listened to tapes, not interested in seeing friends or going to the pit. When Pete asked me about the big night at his apartment, I told him Rob was gone, but that he did have a wonderful time there.

"Friends are hard to lose," he said, "especially when you guys had so much trouble becoming friends in the first place."

Chapter
26

I had no idea how Kelly was going to react to my news. That night in July she greeted me with an innocent smile, her hair braided like the first time we talked in the fourth grade. She led me to her porch swing, and we sat back against the soft pillows.

"Nights like this are wonderful for talks, don't you think?" she asked.

"Well, it depends on what the subject is. Look, I don't know how to tell you, so I guess I'll just say it," I said. "Robbie's gone away. I'm not sure why because he didn't tell me he was going and I haven't heard from him."

"You mean he's gone . . . from East Powell?"

"Yes."

She tried covering her shock by keeping her face expressionless, but I saw something weird fluttering in her throat. She lowered her head. "I can't believe it," she murmured. "He didn't call me. How long has he been gone?"

"Almost two weeks."

"It's . . . incredible. How do you feel?"

"I'm madder than hell at him." Until then I hadn't realized my own anger. He called me a coward all the time, but he ran. Was he afraid to ask for my help or just too proud? "Anyway, I should be glad he's gone because of you. But I'm not. I'm depressed."

Kelly sat up and pressed her palm against her forehead, speaking quietly. "I dreamed that when Robbie grew up and got over some of his problems we'd end up together. That's why I didn't get too upset when he told me we'd better not see each other for a while when he was in the hospital. I hoped we'd belong to each other someday. It sounds so silly when I say it, but it's true. Todd, you don't know how much I care. I've been covering up everything."

Kelly's voice broke. I'd never seen anyone cry like that. She put her arms around me and I hugged her for a long time while it got dark and the only sounds were the crickets and the faraway bark of someone's dog.

After some time she raised her head. Her face looked terrible. "Tell me he'll come back," she said. "I need to hear it."

"I honestly don't know," I said. "Do you want me to lie? Where is that jerk? I ask myself that question every day. What's the baseball team going to do next year? How can Robbie finish school without me after him all the time?"

She wiped her eyes and nodded. "We have to stay good friends, okay—even though I've treated you terribly?"

"Sure, we'll do some things together if you want."

"And have talks. You're my favorite person for that, you know?"

"It's been some year," I said, letting out a huge sigh.

I stayed with her a long time that night. We talked about everything, then just sat and stared into the dark.

The next Sunday Grandpa let me drive his Porsche to Fall Hill. Mom was at an insurance conference in Lake Geneva, only because Stan asked her to go. For once I looked forward to seeing Dad, maybe because I had waited so long between visits. I had an odd, bottled-up sensation that had me pacing around that morning instead of eating breakfast.

When I reached Fall Hill and got to my dad's room, I sat down with him as usual and remained quiet, thinking. Mom said Dad understood what anyone said to him. Now he could listen to me. I had to get it out.

I opened up, really spilling my guts to him, repeating everything that had happened since the day in December when I got hit in the back with a snowball, how I hated Robbie for having Kelly, for his baseball ability, for taking over managing the basketball team, for getting in good with Grandpa.

I described the fight and how I felt afterward, how I almost didn't make the team, about Rob and me becoming friends, the crazy times we had, his accident, the afternoon I found out about his dad. I ended with the dance and Pete's apartment and how I lost my nerve when Rob didn't, and how he disappeared the next day.

"I guess having a friend like Robbie helped me, Dad, when I felt bad about you being here. He always told me

ou'd be okay. He was so funny. He had a grin that
ould crack a mirror, but the girls liked it. Now he's
one. Oh, I have plenty of other friends. Grandpa can't
ait to get back to the farm. He misses it, and I'm going
 miss him.

"So that leaves Mom and me. She's working so hard at
he agency. You'd be proud of her. I sure am. But she
ates it. She doesn't complain, though, because she's
oing it for you."

I hesitated, staring at his passive face. "Dad, I don't
are if you work just as hard as you used to, or if you
on't work at all, or if you don't have time to talk to me.
ll accept that. I know now that you worked hard so you
ould give me the things I wanted. I feel bad that I didn't
ealize it. I respect you. I always have. I mean, I'm like
ou, one of those worriers. I'll probably go bald, and I
ight even have to get a pacemaker, but those things
on't scare me anymore. I just wish—please don't leave
e like he did. He must have a good reason for not
oming back, but, Dad, you don't. Mom and I need
ou."

I said most of the last part with my head down. I felt at
eace having said all of it.

Raising my head, I looked at Dad. He blinked. Tears
ere rolling down his gray, lined face. "Dad, what's the
atter?" I asked, frightened. His mouth moved.
What?" I leaned toward him.

"I . . . won't leave," he said faintly.

"You won't leave Fall Hill? Oh, please, Dad, don't say
at."

"No. I won't leave you," he said. ". . . Been gone too

187

long . . ." Slowly, he reached his hands toward me.

When I got home that night I was so charged I ran up to Grandpa's room three steps at a time and barged through his door, scaring the heck out of him. "Grandpa, Dad talked to me tonight!" I cried. I should have told Mom first, but she was probably sleeping off her trip.

"You're kidding," he said, walking toward me. "What did he say?"

"That he wanted to come home."

"He might have been talking to the wall."

"No. No, he really talked to me. I was telling him all about Rob and me, and then I said I didn't want him to leave me, too, and he said he wouldn't. Then he talked a little more and I told him we'd all help. I went to the staff doctor and he said it was some sort of progress. Grandpa, Dad wants you and Mom to visit."

Grandpa got off his bed, grabbed my shoulders and gave me the biggest hug I've ever had in my life. "You wonderful kid!" he hollered.

Our excitement brought Mom to the third floor. "What is this?" she asked.

"You'll never believe it," Grandpa said, dancing around the room in front of the sexy posters Robbie had drawn for him. "Annie darling, this is your happy day."

"What," she asked, pointing to the pictures, "are *those?*"

Chapter
27

After a few days we learned Dad had begun to face things he'd blocked out for months. I can't take credit for his recovery. Maybe I talked to him about the right subject at the zero hour. Maybe he had a friend like Rob when he was young. Maybe he was just tired of being alone. As Grandpa said, "If I were God, I'd know."

Grandpa announced he'd be going back to the farm as soon as Dad came home and got back to work, which meant sometime the next spring. He asked me to spend another summer with him.

The days passed lazily until Pete got me a job at A & L taking inventory and selling parts. I began to learn auto mechanics, and although I wasn't a whiz, I enjoyed getting my hands oily and my brain involved in a new skill.

I purposely stayed away from Kelly. I needed to settle feelings for her inside myself first. Oddly enough, I missed Diane and planned to write her a letter before long, if I ever got all the grease off my fingers.

One day in August when I picked up our mail, I found a postcard in the bottom of our mailbox for me. On the front was a picture of the business district of some town in Indiana. The postcard had fold lines and was frayed at the edges as if someone had forgotten to mail it for a long time. I knew immediately it was from Robbie. I turned it over and realized with a start that after everything that had happened between us, I had never seen his handwriting before. Like his purple baseball hat, it looked terrible.

Todd,

Dad broke his promise again, but this time he went too far. He found the money I was saving to find my mom and blew it. That was the last straw. He'll never change and I want something else. I did have a little more money hidden somewhere else, and I took it and hit the road. She's out there somewhere and I'm going to find her. Don't worry about me. You're a good guy.

> *Your friend,*
> *Rob*

P.S. I didn't do IT either that night. Ha! Ha!

I sat holding the crumpled postcard for a long time, laughing until I cried.

Chapter
28

Yesterday, while going through some notebooks and papers to get ready for the move to California, I remembered the twenty-dollar bill I had slipped between the pages of my Bible over two years ago. I smiled when I thought of why I had put it there.

I heard my dad calling to me from the bottom of the stairs. He, Mom and I were going to Bernie's Bowl for hamburgers in a few minutes. After retiring with relief from the agency, my mother had gone back to Best's two days a week. Couldn't get over those bargain prices, I guess.

I glanced across my room at the light filtering under the shade the same way it did the afternoon Robbie told me the truth about his family. I sighed. That was some afternoon. Some year. Some friendship.

I thought about Kelly. I guess I knew we would never be together, but our relationship had changed me. She'll always be a part of my life. But then, they all will: Robbie, Rick, even Diane.

"Todd, are you coming?" Same old Dad, impatient as ever.

Grabbing my jacket, I stuffed the twenty in my pocket and took the stairs two at a time, hoping Dad would let me pay for the meal.